PASSAGE OF TIME

When charismatic Josh Stephens literally blows into her life, Melanie Treloar finds him a disturbing presence in the hostel she runs in west Cornwall. During his job of assessing some old mining remains Josh discovers a sea cave that holds an intriguing secret. When he is caught in a cliff fall — saving Melanie's niece — it is Melanie who comes to his rescue. Although this puts their relationship on a new level, can they solve the many problems that still remain?

SPECIAL MESSAGE TO F

THE ULVERSCROFT FOU
(registered UK charity num

was established in 1972 to prov
search, diagnosis and treatment
    Examples of major projects
     the Ulverscroft Foundati

The Children's Eye Unit at
Hospital, London
The Ulverscroft Children's F
Ormond Street Hospital for
Funding research into e
treatment at the Department
University of Leicester
The Ulverscroft Vision
Institute of Child Health
Twin operating theatres
Ophthalmic Hospital, Lond
The Chair of Ophthalmo
Australian College of Opht

u can help further the work
  by making a donation or 1
very contribution is gratefu
ould like to help support 1
require further information

THE ULVERSCROFT
The Green, Bradgate
Leicester LE7 7FU
Tel: (0116) 23

ebsite: www.foundation

29/11/13.

14/12/13.
20/12/13.
9/1/14.

Spencer

FROST
HOUGHTON

Pleas
date sh

Northam

w

JANET THOMAS

PASSAGE OF TIME

Complete and Unabridged

LINFORD
Leicester

First published in Great Britain in 2012

First Linford Edition
published 2013

A catalogue record for this book is available
from the British Library.

ISBN 978–1–4448–1649–5

Published by
F. A. Thorpe (Publishing)
Anstey, Leicestershire

Set by Words & Graphics Ltd.
Anstey, Leicestershire
Printed and bound in Great Britain by
T. J. International Ltd., Padstow, Cornwall

This book is printed on acid-free paper

1

The telephone in reception rang just as I had dropped into a chair and taken the first sip of a well-earned cup of coffee.

'I'll get that, Claire,' I called to my sister, who I could see through the patio doors, was still working away outside. With a groan and a sigh I rose to my tired feet again and headed down the passage.

On the way, I caught a glimpse through the window of our signboard swinging in the ever-present wind from the sea. *Carn Dhu Backpackers' Hostel.* Even after two years I still felt a little quiver of excitement, as I always did when I thought of this business venture into which we had sunk all our savings, along with our hopes and dreams. Pride too, that it was doing so well, although still in its infancy.

'Another reservation, was it?' I met Claire coming down the corridor towards me.

'Yes, a couple of ramblers wanting the weekend before Easter.' I smiled and ran a hand through my short blonde crop. 'We're almost fully booked straight through, now.'

'Great — we'll have to build on an annexe at this rate!'

★ ★ ★

By the following afternoon, the March wind that had been blowing steadily all day around this exposed peninsula, was gathering force. It was screaming angrily around the crags of Carn Dhu, the towering rocky outcrop that loomed behind the house, and battering the huddle of long-abandoned mine workings at its foot. Far below, the sea was being whipped up into peaks and ridges crested with white foam.

I was looking anxiously out of the window at our signboard, fearful for its

2

safety as it creaked and swung furiously on its hinges, when I saw Claire draw up in the car.

'Ugh, it's tipping down out there now.' She appeared at the back door, loaded with shopping bags. 'It started raining just as I left Penzance.' She stomped into the kitchen and shook her wet hair out of her eyes. 'There's some more stuff still in the car. I'll take this lot down to Carol.'

Carol was our cook, cleaner, general help and friend. The only domestic staff we could afford to employ, she was worth her weight in gold.

Claire and I shared the administration, the general running of the place and the sorting out of problems as they arose. Rob her husband, being a capable handyman, looked after the practical maintenance of the place, indoors and out, in his spare time, as well as working for a local building firm.

'I'll get the rest,' I called, as I threw a coat over my head and crossed the yard.

But something caught my attention out at sea, and I shaded my eyes to peer through the driving rain.

Yes, there was a fishing boat out there, tossing about on the heaving sea. I watched as it dipped and rose in the mighty troughs and peaks. Was it in trouble? It didn't seem to be making much headway, although how could it in conditions like this? But surely, it was drifting in towards the land, wasn't it?

The stricken boat held my attention and in spite of the weather, I couldn't take my eyes off it. I wrapped my anorak closer around me and watched.

Below where the hostel stood was a small cove, where if he could make it, the fisherman would find shelter, but there was a perilous reef of rocks at the entrance. If he came too close to that, both he and his boat would be in real danger.

I turned and ran back to the house. 'Rob! Rob! Come quickly — there's a boat in trouble out in the bay.'

Rob appeared, ducking his head to

avoid the low doorway. He was a giant of a man, solid, capable and usually unflappable, and we relied on him totally for all of our practical problems.

'A boat? Where? Show me.'

We ran outside and I pointed as the boat lurched into view.

'I see it.' Rob nodded briefly and turned on a heel. 'Right. You go and phone the coastguard. I'll get some rope and stuff from the shed, and get down there.'

'No, wait! I'm coming with you.' I ran back to the house and grabbed some over-trousers and a waterproof jacket, swiftly pulling them on and stuffing my feet into Wellingtons.

'No. No Mel,' Rob shouted above the wind. 'You stay here — it's too dangerous.'

Ignoring him, I turned to Claire. 'You'll tell the coastguard, won't you?'

'You're going, then?' Claire bit her lip. 'Oh, do be careful, both of you!' She knew the tortuous track leading down the cliff face to the cove as well as I did.

We'd been scrambling up and down there since childhood.

Difficult to negotiate in good weather, now in wet and slippery conditions with darkness closing in, one wrong step would be all it took for us to have a casualty on our hands. But Rob needed help — he'd never manage on his own. Besides which, I was a trained nurse — there could well be injured men on board. Swallowing down my own terror, I took a deep breath and stepped outside.

A blast of wind caught me sideways and I followed him towards the shed.

'Get blankets ready and boil up some water. Make tea — soup — anything hot,' Rob was shouting over his shoulder to Claire. He emerged clad in waterproofs and rubber waders, with a rope slung around one shoulder and a massive torch in his hand.

He jumped as he caught sight of me in the doorway, but made nothing of it.

'Give me the torch,' I said, tugging it

from his grasp. 'That'll free up one of your hands.'

He nodded briefly, then set off at a lope down the lane. I caught him up at the edge of the cliff, before we both descended into the all-enveloping greyness of sea and sky.

The powerful torch cast a welcome beam as we negotiated the narrow track, Rob leading the way, more sure-footed than I was. I stumbled along in his wake, my free hand clutching at heather bushes and tussocks of grass to steady myself as the blustery wind threatened to blow us off course.

But at last we reached the bottom. The rain seemed to be easing off, but not for long. A rank of menacing, big-bellied clouds were still marching in from the west.

I followed Rob across the slippery, weed-covered rocks, clutching at his jacket as a sudden gust caught me by surprise and I lurched perilously close to the edge.

'All right, Mel?' he called above the noise of the crashing waves. Pounding against the reef, they were throwing huge fountains of foam high in the air, before the rip tide sucked the water backwards, dragging a clattering mass of stones with it.

'Don't you come any further.' Rob's tone was terse. 'Just stay here and hold that torch steady. I'm going out towards the boat.' He jumped off the last big rock and started wading thigh-deep through the surging water.

Ignoring what Rob had told me, I followed him to the edge of the reef. He was only thinking of my safety. But he would need the torch's light and I was too far away here.

I took a few more steps. And now I could see how close the stricken boat was. Dangerously close, helpless against the wind and the buffeting waves that together would batter it to pieces.

Rob had braced his back against an isolated pillar of rock. Uncoiling the rope, he looped it round his waist and tied it firmly. Instinctively I held the torch higher and swung it to alert the men in the boat. At that moment Rob took aim and tossed the end of the line towards them. The wind snatched it away. It fell uselessly back into the angry water as the boat was tossed high on a huge breaker, then plunged back into the swell.

My heart began to pound against my ribs. Were we attempting the impossible? With my forearm I wiped the damp spray from my face and tasted salt on my tongue. The tail-end of the last surge splashed high over the rock beside me, and soaked me to the waist, the run-off from it filling my boots.

But I hardly noticed. And I'd lost all feeling in my hands as I clenched them around the torch, terrified I would drop it. I gazed, mesmerised at Rob. He was a big man but now, dwarfed by the magnitude of wind and water, he seemed no more than a puppet.

Quick, Rob, try again before the next wave! I held my breath and silently urged him on. And this time . . . this time . . . yes! He'd done it. One of the men had grabbed it and was making it fast to the boat. With a huge sigh of relief I let out all my breath in a silent whoop of triumph.

'Mel! Over here!' Rob was waving an arm to me. I scrambled over the remaining rocks and stepped into the water. It was only knee-height now. The tide must be going out. Yes. A patch of wet sand was showing at the entrance to the cove.

'Help me tow them in,' he grunted, taking the torch from me and clipping it to his waistband. I stepped in front of him and gripped the sodden rope with both hands. It slipped uselessly through my icy fingers. Ignoring the pain as the rope burned them back to life, I pulled with all my strength.

Between us we managed to guide the boat towards the break in the reef, and as it cleared the remaining rocks, the two crewmen jumped out and began to haul it in.

'Drop the rope now, Mel. We'll do it by hand.' Puffing and panting, between us we managed to drag the boat up the beach.

'Just a bit further,' someone said. 'Get it above the tideline and we'll be OK.'

'Rob, look!' I pointed. 'Over there. The inshore lifeboat's coming. That was quick.' As I straightened, I could see the bright orange of the rescue vessel.

'He'll have come out of Sennen,' Rob grunted. 'Blown by the wind in his back. Too late for us, though.'

The vessel paused and a crewman with a loudhailer called out something I didn't catch. Rob went back to the edge of the water and with shouts and gestures indicated that we were all right. The lifeboat started up again, turned, and went on its way.

'That was well done, my handsome.' Rob turned to me and clapped me on the shoulder as the two crewmen turned back to check the damaged boat, talking among themselves. 'You get back now and tell them we're on our way. Just got to make sure things are secure down here, then we'll be right behind you.'

He paused and unfastened the torch from his belt. 'Here, you take this. We can manage. Look.' He pointed to the sky. The storm was clearing at last and a watery moon was riding through the remaining clouds.

I dragged myself up the cliff, ignoring the water sloshing about in my boots. I was too exhausted to empty them. If I stopped now I'd never get going again.

* * *

'What happened? Where's Rob?' Claire came running across the yard to meet me. 'Are you all right? Both of you?'

'Fine, everything's fine.' I summoned up a smile. 'They're on their way up now. Two fishermen and Rob. Get the kettle on while I go and change.'

I dumped all my dripping clothing in the porch and dashed upstairs. Under the quickest shower I'd ever had, I thawed out, dressed in record time and was downstairs again just as the rumble of voices outside told me the men had arrived.

'Oh, Rob, are you all right?' Claire anxiously ran to meet her husband. 'Not hurt? Er, any of you, that is?' she added, turning to the others and ushering them inside.

Soon the kitchen seemed to be full of large, wet men, and the entry porch piled high with streaming waterproofs and boots.

'No, we're all OK, my handsome.' He waved the others to chairs around the big central table. 'Ah, we're ready for some of that tea.' He grinned across at his wife as she was filling large mugs and piling a plate with Carol's saffron buns.

'Now, this chap here is Chris.' Rob started on the introductions, indicating a brawny and weather-beaten middle-aged man with fists like small hams and a magnificent beard. 'The boat belongs to him. Claire, my wife,' he pointed, as Chris nodded and smiled.

'Hello.' Claire looked over her shoulder and reached for spoons and sugar.

Rob waved a hand towards the other, younger man who was still hovering in the doorway.

'Come on in boy, and get warmed up,' he said to him, beckoning as the man stepped forward into the kitchen.

Up to now I'd only been able to make out a tall male figure silhouetted against the light from the entry, where he was hanging up his wet jacket. Then as he came forward, I could see him properly. He was smiling and I had to stifle a gasp, for here was the most arresting man I had ever seen.

Lean, wiry build. Glossy dark hair, soaked and dishevelled, tumbling over a high forehead. Rugged good looks. Impish grin, teeth gleaming very white in a narrow, sensitive face. But it was the eyes that were heart-stopping. Pools of melting dark chocolate flecked with motes of gold, they lit up as he spoke.

'I'm Josh Stephens.' He extended a hand and grasped mine firmly. 'You're Mel, I think. Right?'

But I'd flinched as pain shot through my scraped and swollen palm. Clearly startled, he turned it over, then reached for the other one.

'Oh, I'm so sorry,' he said gently. 'I didn't realise.'

'It was the rope,' I replied, flushing as he bent to take a closer look and his curly hair brushed my cheek. 'I'll put something on them in a minute.'

'You were very brave.' The stunning eyes were full of sympathy and I felt another wave of colour creeping up my neck.

He was wearing a blue sweater over a T-shirt, both of which were sodden in spite of the hooded jacket which was dripping on a peg out in the porch. I was slightly mystified. This man didn't look a bit like a fisherman, his hand had been smooth to my touch, and he'd obviously not been wearing water-proofs.

Confused as he smiled down at me, but not knowing why, I said the first thing that came into my head.

'Oh, look, you must take off your clothes!' I blurted. Then, realising how it sounded, I hastily added the rest of it. 'You're soaked through.'

But it was too late. Chris had let out an enormous guffaw, Rob was smirking to himself and Claire's jaw had dropped in disbelief. And worst of all, those arresting eyes still looking into mine were twinkling with suppressed mirth as his mouth creased into an even broader smile.

I could feel my face flaming now. For goodness sake, why was this man having such an effect on me? Here I was, a competent businesswoman, totally used to dealing with people. I just didn't blurt out remarks like that without thinking. Where had it all come from?

Lost in confusion, I heard myself babbling away non-stop, only making things worse. About borrowing from

Rob while we put his own things through the tumble dryer. About coming to sit beside the Aga and get warm after he'd changed. Anything to cover the effect his proximity was having on me, and the enormously embarrassing gaffe I'd made.

But eventually everything settled down. Josh came back wearing a pair of Rob's jeans which would have gone twice around him, cinched in with a belt, and a sweater with arms so long he had had to roll them up to his elbows.

The resulting laughter drove away the last of my embarrassment. After that, we drew the thick curtains against the darkness outside, then relaxed and warmed through, we were ready to listen as the visitors told us the whole of their dramatic tale.

2

'Out fishing, were you?' Rob turned to the boat's skipper, Chris, and arched a brow.

'Not this time, no. It was like this, see.' Chris took a large swig of tea and held out his mug with a smile for me to refill. 'Thanks, my handsome.' He leaned back and folded his arms.

'I was taking Josh here, out to have a look along the coast from the seaward side. For his job, see.'

Everyone turned to look at Josh.

'I'm a geophysicist,' he explained, looking at our blank expressions. 'It's a kind of surveyor,' he added with a smile. 'At the moment the firm I'm working for wants to explore the old mine workings of Wheal Hope over there,' he nodded towards the window, 'with a view to possibly re-opening it.'

'Wheal Hope?' My jaw dropped,

seeing in my mind's eye the clutter of abandoned workings I'd been accustomed to all my life. 'But that was closed down over a hundred years ago!'

'I know.' Josh glanced across the table at me. 'But only because the price of tin and copper dropped so sharply during that big slump.' He raised an expressive hand. 'I've spoken to men whose fathers can remember that time, and they say there was plenty of ore left underground there. It just wasn't worth bringing it up.'

'So why are your employers so interested in it now, after all this time?' Claire gave him a puzzled look as she drained her tea and reached for a saffron bun.

'Because the price of tin has just rocketed lately, and they want to see how viable it would be to drain the workings and do a proper survey of them. Modern machinery can do so much more than the old men were able to.'

'So Josh asked me to take him out in

the boat and look at the cliffs for signs of the old adits,' Chris chipped in.

'Adits are drainage channels or entrances,' Josh murmured. 'Sometimes they are still visible as holes in the cliffs.'

'When we came out of Hayle the sun was shining,' Chris went on. 'Bit windy, but we didn't take no notice of that. Then this squall came up and the Cornish Maid started pitching and tossing like a cork, just when we was rounding the headland down below here.' He jerked a thumb. 'Next thing I know, the damn engine cut out and we was drifting. Being driven in towards the rocks, we was, weren't we, Josh?' He glanced towards the younger man, who nodded.

'Yes, it was a bit hair-raising for a minute or two.' His eyes were solemn, obviously reliving the experience. 'Until we noticed your signal, and then saw Rob here scrambling out towards us. I've never been so pleased to see other human beings in my life!' He grinned at

Rob. 'Especially one with a guiding light and the other with a rope in his hands.'

'That was Mel with the light.' Rob turned to me and briefly patted my arm. 'Couldn't have managed without her as it happened.' I took it as an admission I'd been right to disobey his orders, and smiled.

'We saw the boat from up here,' I put in, 'and called Rob. I came with him to hold the torch, then stood there with my heart in my mouth, willing him on. It was an unbelieveable drama.'

'It certainly was,' Josh agreed. 'You were very brave, Mel.' His eyes held mine for a moment and I thought yet again what an attractive man he was. 'And she was the only one of us who was hurt. To damage her hands on the rope like that seems hardly fair!'

I felt my cheeks colour as he glanced back at me with concern on his face.

'Oh, I've put some ointment on them — they're not too bad now,' I replied, playing it down.

'Well, I must phone my missus and tell her what has happened and where I am.' Chris pushed back his chair and rose. 'She'll drive over and pick me up. Then I'll come back in daylight with a couple of mates and get the boat started. Do you mind if I use your phone?' He looked over my way.

'Of course.' I nodded as Rob got to his feet, too.

'I'll show you where it is.' Rob led the way to the reception area at the front of the house.

'Never could get on with they mobile things,' Chris muttered as they left the room. 'I've got one but can't get no signal on it half the time. Tried to when we was in trouble, but the cliffs are too high. They do make it cut out.'

* * *

'Will Chris and his wife take you back, too, Josh?' I asked while the other men were out of the room.

The younger man looked a little uncomfortable. 'Well,' he raised his shoulders and spread his hands helplessly, 'I can hardly go out in these, can I?' He stood up and as Claire and I looked at him we both burst out laughing.

He was still wearing Rob's oversized clothes, of course.

'Oh, dear!' Claire shook her head and chuckled. 'No, definitely not!'

'Do you live in Hayle?' I enquired.

Josh shook his head. 'No, I'm staying a bit further up the coast. I'm in a B&B at Portreath, while this job lasts.'

'In that case, I suggest you stay here for the night. We've got plenty of empty beds still. There are only a couple of birdwatchers here at the moment.' I smiled. 'And Rob can fix you up with a nice big pair of pyjamas.'

His broad answering smile seemed to light up the room. 'Well, if you're sure, that would be very nice, thanks.'

'Good. Then one of us will drive you

back to Portreath in the morning. If you come this way I'll show you where you'll be sleeping tonight.'

★   ★   ★

I was very conscious of Josh's height towering over my own five feet four, as he followed me up the stairs, and I started talking like something wound up, as I usually did when not feeling totally at ease.

'The men's dormitory is on the second floor, facing the front, so you'll have a good view of the sea in the morning.'

I kept on talking as we reached the landing. 'Our guests share the showers with the other rooms on this floor. They're at the end of the passage down there.' I pointed.

'The communal kitchen/diner and lounge are on the right as you come downstairs. That's where the two men who are staying at the moment will be. There are coffee and tea-making facilities there.' I paused to draw breath. 'Of course our private wing, where we've just come from, is quite separate.'

'You must get very busy in the summer. This is a lovely spot — in daylight and good weather, that is.' Josh paused to peer out of the window and I joined him.

The rain had passed over now but there was still a stiff breeze blowing. The moon had strengthened, and above the sea it was riding high, seemingly driven along by rags of clouds streaming in from the west.

I drew away and pushed open the door to the dormitory. 'Oh, we do. And we certainly need the business.'

'How long have you been open? I've never come across this place before. And I've done a fair bit of walking around here in the past.' He turned from the window and followed me inside.

'Only a couple of years. But this was our childhood home, Claire's and mine, and our other sister, Alex,' I explained.

Josh raised an eyebrow and looked around appraisingly at the sloping ceiling and thick cob walls. 'Really? And you've always lived here?'

'Well, not exactly.' However, I couldn't explain all that to a total stranger, nor did I want to. 'But it's a long story.' We had stopped in the middle of the room while Josh took another long look around.

'It's a really interesting building. Was it attached to the mine years ago?'

'Yes, it was the original count-house.' I crossed to the window and pulled the red-striped curtains across to shut out the darkness. 'More accurately, the account house,' I added over my shoulder.

'Ah, yes. Where the shareholders — or 'adventurers' held their monthly dinners and counted up their profits!' Josh grinned as I turned back to him.

'Of course, I forgot you know all about it.' As I smiled, our eyes met and I moved away to break the contact, which was having the strangest effect on me.

'I must go and get some bed linen and pillows,' I said abruptly. 'The cupboard's just out here on the landing.'

Josh hung about as I made up the bed. When he noticed how my sore fingers were hampering me, he rolled up his overlong sleeves and helped me tuck in the bottom sheet.

It was a thoughtful gesture; not many men would have been so perceptive. He dealt neatly with the corners as if he did this job all the time, and I wondered whether he had a wife or partner. But I could hardly ask him outright. I was pretty sure he would be in a relationship of some kind. Men with the charisma of Josh Stephens were never short of a female companion. But it was totally none of my business.

I thumped a pillow harder than was strictly necessary and tossed it toward the head of the bed. Josh neatly fended it with one hand and smoothed it into place.

'There you are then.' I stood back as we finished, and turned to go. 'I'll send Rob up in a minute with some things for you.'

'Thanks, Mel. I really appreciate it.' Josh sat down on the newly-made bed and bounced gently on the mattress. 'This feels really comfortable.'

I waved a dismissive hand. 'You're welcome,' I replied formally. 'I'll see you for breakfast in the morning. Sleep well.'

'I will. I'm whacked,' he replied. 'And I'm sure you are too. Goodnight, then.'

I could feel his gaze still following me as I left the room and headed for the stairs.

★   ★   ★

The next morning dawned crisp and clear. The sea was at its picturesque best, a sheet of periwinkle blue stretching as far as the eye could see. I was at the kitchen window, glancing at the sky to see if the day was going to remain as good as it seemed, when a voice at my elbow startled me and I whirled around to find Josh Stephens at my side.

'It's looking a bit different out there from yesterday.' He gave me his heart-stopping smile. I noticed he had retrieved his own clothes and was back in jeans and a sweater.

'So are you!' I returned the smile as I looked him up and down. 'But yes, it seems settled for the time being.'

'And how are your hands today?' he asked politely, holding my gaze.

'Oh, much better, pretty well back to normal. See?' I opened my palms to show him. To my surprise he took them gently in his own, rubbing his thumbs gently over the tender areas.

I hadn't been prepared for the knee-jerk reaction that came with his touch, or the melting sensation deep inside me. Flustered, I broke the eye contact and removed my hands as soon as I could.

'Oh, yes. Good. The redness has faded and that swelling's gone down completely.' He smiled. 'I hated the feeling you'd got hurt on my account.'

I started. Surely he must be joking? But his face was serious.

'Impressive view you've got from here.' Josh turned and leaned his forearms on the windowsill, scanning the broad sweep of the Atlantic. He craned forward to peer in the other direction and take in the towering rock piles behind the house where they thrust upwards to pierce the sky.

'A position like this has to be good for your business. What sort of people do you get? Ramblers mostly, I suppose.'

'Yes, we do get a lot of walkers, certainly, but also birdwatchers, botanists, rock climbers, artists and people interested in the mining remains. And as we're the only 'comfort stop' for miles around,' I said with a chuckle, 'most of them either stay with us or at least drop in for refreshments during their visit to the area.'

'I see. So there's quite a lot on offer for anyone on holiday.'

'Oh, absolutely. Now, breakfast?' I pointed. 'There's coffee on top of the Aga. Cereal, toast or a full English if you'd like it.'

He poured himself a mug of coffee, then folded his long legs beneath the table. 'Cereal and toast will be fine, thanks.'

'In that case, choose what you want. It's all in front of you. The toaster's over there.'

'Where is everybody?' Josh took a miniature box and broke it open.

I sat down at the other end of the table and buttered a roll. 'Rob's gone to get the car out. He's on his way to work — with a building firm in Hayle.' I reached for the marmalade. 'Claire was up early, she's outside pegging washing on the line. Carol will be here in a minute.'

'Um, Mel, I was thinking.' Josh looked up and stopped crunching cereal.

'Mmm?' I glanced towards him and raised an eyebrow.

'Now that I've found this place of yours, it seems to me it would be far more convenient for me to stay here than at Portreath. Ideal, in fact.' He spread his hands eloquently. 'Right on top of my work. What do you think? Could I be a paying guest for a few weeks?'

'Of course. What a good idea!' I felt my spirits give a little lift. It must have been the sudden ray of sunshine slanting through the window.

'In that case, Josh . . . excuse me a minute, I'll try and catch Rob before he goes.' I jumped up and was halfway across the kitchen, calling over my shoulder as I went.

'He could give you a lift into Hayle. You can catch a bus to Portreath from there and pick up your things and your car. OK?'

By the time I returned, Josh was flinging on his jacket and coming out to meet me.

'It's all right, I've caught him. He'd been helping Claire fix up the washing line, and was just starting the car.'

'Phew! That was close then. Thanks, Mel. Brilliant idea. See you later.'

★　★　★

When I returned to the kitchen after working upstairs, where I'd been hanging fresh curtains ready for the new season, I found Claire bent over a pile of cardboard boxes and carrier bags. She looked up as I came in.

'This lot is the rest of the stuff I bought in Penzance yesterday. Carol didn't have time, it's her half day, so I said I'd put it away.'

'I'll help you. Isn't it amazing how much we need at the beginning of a season? Although some of it is for the residents' kitchen as well. But actually,' I glanced at my watch, 'it's coming up to lunchtime, and I'm starving. Aren't you?'

Claire nodded.

'OK, I'll see to it while you finish that box you're on. Leave the rest for later. What shall we have to eat?' I pulled open the door of the fridge and peered inside. 'Ham and salad all right? Oh, and there's the soup that we didn't use last night, when we thought there might be several men on the boat.'

'Whatever. That's fine by me.' My sister straightened and tossed back her shoulder length hair, tangled by the persistent sea breeze that was always blowing at the height where we lived.

She ran an impatient hand through her thick tresses. 'Oh, I don't know why I bother trying to keep this tidy. It never stays in one place. Rob likes it long, otherwise I'd have had it cut short ages ago, like yours.'

'Oh, you know long hair's never been my thing. Cropped like this it was easier to wear under my cap when I was nursing.'

I slapped two plates on the worktop and buttered the rolls.

'Do you ever hear from 'Dr David' at all now?' Claire reached round me to put some tins in the cupboard above my head.

'No.' My hands stilled as I was jerked back to my previous life in a busy hospital in Middlesex. 'He gave up replying to my messages a few months after I came back here. I was kept so busy looking after Mum, and with you ill too, I didn't have time to think about him then.'

'But now? You miss him, don't you? And you must miss the nursing. I've seen you daydreaming, with that look on your face ... ?' She raised an eyebrow.

I shrugged. 'When Mum recovered and moved into her flat and I had time to think again, then yes, I did miss him, badly. I truly loved him, Claire. At first, that is.' Even now there was a catch in my voice. She reached out her free hand and patted my arm in sympathy.

I picked up a bottle of salad dressing and shook it violently. 'And I was so hurt, humiliated and just plain mad at the way he treated me, I couldn't get him out of my head.' The top flew off the bottle and I swore under my breath as I grabbed a roll of kitchen paper.

'But since we got this venture off the ground, I've become so bound up with it that honestly Claire, I would never go back to nursing now, even though I was doing so well in my career. And I shall never, never trust any man again.'

'Never is a long time, Mel. You're still young. You could easily meet someone else. And I really hope you will. You deserve to be happy, with a life of your own, instead of always looking after other people.'

'Huh. Twenty-eight is hardly young.' I slapped slices of ham onto the bread and half-turned towards her. 'Oh, Claire, you're so lucky to have met a man like Rob.'

Her face was solemn. 'I know. I do realise that. He's a gem.' She sighed. 'If only we could . . . '

'Have a family,' I finished for her. 'And I'm sure it will happen for you, even after the disappointments you've had.'

Claire shrugged and I began slicing tomatoes.

'As for me, I realise how much I've loved this house, and this bit of Cornwall, ever since we were all children. Sometimes I think I could spend the rest of my life here. Certainly I could never face living in a city again.' I pointed with the knife for emphasis.

'Hey, watch what you're doing with that thing!' Claire gently pushed it away from her with a finger.

'Oops, sorry! I was daydreaming. This is ready now.' She joined me at the breakfast bar and we sat down to eat.

I'd hardly started when we heard the phone ringing and both moved together. 'I'll get it,' I said, pushing Claire back into her seat as I headed towards reception.

'Oh, Alex, hello.' I picked up the receiver to hear the familiar voice of our youngest sister. 'Fine thanks. And you?' The formalities over, I sat down to listen to what she was saying.

'Really?' I felt my brows rise. 'From Easter onwards, for the whole summer? Well, yes, I suppose so. If you're sure you're willing to lend a hand. We're booked solid and it's going to be all go for a few months. It is already, in fact, with Easter not far away. We'll be opening up properly then. We've had a few winter visitors, but nothing like it will be then — I hope!'

We finished the call and I wandered thoughtfully back to my interrupted lunch. Claire looked up expectantly as I entered the room. 'Another booking?'

'No. No, it wasn't an enquiry — well not in the sense you mean. It was Alex this time.'

'Alex?' Claire's eyes widened. 'What did she want, anything particular or just a chat? How are they all?'

'Yes, fine. But apparently Andy has to

go abroad to work for a few months over the summer. Alex wonders if she and Isobel can come and stay here while he's away. She made it plain that she's willing to pull her weight and not be a bother to us.'

Claire, whose brow had creased at the mention of Alex, now relaxed and gave a nod. 'Oh, well, in that case . . . but I hope you made it clear how busy we're likely to be.'

'I certainly did. And remember, she's not as feckless as she used to be, Claire. Marriage and motherhood changed all that, didn't it?'

Claire nodded and shook back her long blonde hair. We were both fair, and blue-eyed like our mother. Alex was very different, having inherited our father's dark colouring. Different in character too, having been a bit of a rebel in her youth.

'When's she coming?' Claire stood up, yawned and stretched her arms.

'In about a fortnight. She'll phone us again before then.'

★ ★ ★

We were just clearing the dishes when I heard a car draw up outside and glancing out of the window, saw Josh Stephens unloading several boxes and bags from the boot.

'He seems to have a lot of stuff,' Claire remarked through a mouthful of salad.

'I expect he's got all sorts of specialist equipment he needs for his surveying.' I watched him staggering towards the door with an armload. He placed his burden inside the porch and went back for the rest.

I pushed back my empty plate. 'I've finished here. I'll go out and give him a hand.'

I crossed the yard to his parked car. 'Hi, Josh, shall I help carry in some of those things?'

'Oh, Mel.' He looked round from the open boot and smiled. 'That would be great. Actually,' he paused, his hand on the top of the door, 'I've been wondering, and I was going to ask you . . . Do you have any single rooms at all?' He spread his hands, indicating the baggage at his feet.

'I wouldn't mind paying a bit more for the privacy. I've got a lot of stuff here to keep under the bed. And, um, some of these instruments are valuable, you see, and they don't all belong to me, but the firm. Not that I'd think for a minute . . . '

I saved him the embarrassment. 'We do have a couple, yes. They're occupied at the moment, and booked up after that, but you're welcome to have one as soon as it's free. I could make sure it's available for as long as you need it after that.'

'Wonderful!' A smile like the sunshine around us lit up his face. 'That would be fantastic.' He lifted out a cardboard box, placed it on the ground with the rest and closed the boot. I picked up one of the large hold-alls and headed indoors.

However, my eyes were dazzled after

the brightness outside and I couldn't for a moment see where I was going. Consequently, I caught my toe on the corner of a box he'd already brought in. Losing my balance I staggered, then went down with a sickening thud, cracking my head on the metal stand of potted plants below the window.

'Ooh . . . ' I groaned, attempting to get to my feet, but sinking to the floor again as I clapped a hand to my temple.

I had heard the expression 'seeing stars', but had never experienced it until now. As my head swam however, I soon learnt how true it was. Coloured dots of light were literally floating around in front of my eyes and the room was spinning. With another groan, I sank onto my knees as darts of pain shot through my skull.

'Mel! Good grief, what on earth . . . ? Here, let me.' Josh extended a hand. 'Try and get up. Slowly now!' he said as I winced at the movement.

I was only partly conscious of the anxious face peering into mine, and of his strong arm under my elbow as he supported my weight.

'N . . . no . . . I can manage . . . ' I raised a feeble hand, but a wave of dizziness stopped the words in my mouth.

'Of course you can't. Here . . . ' To my embarrassment he put one arm around my waist, the other under my legs, lifted me off the ground as if I weighed nothing, and carried me across the passage towards the sitting-room.

There was a waft of spicy aftershave about him, coupled with the scent of his fresh cotton shirt and a faint hint of male sweat. The same aftershave that David used. Through the muzzy haze in my head I smiled. I was in his arms again, my cheek resting against his chest, my head cradled against his warm neck. How I'd missed this closeness. I sighed with contentment.

3

As Josh coughed and cleared his throat, I was jerked back to my senses quicker than by a shower of icy water. I tried to raise my head, and everything spun round me again. But dizzy or not, how could I have been so foolish!

Josh carried me across to the settee that stood under the window, and gently placed me on it. Then, tipping up my chin with one long finger, he touched the sore place with his other hand. I flinched and caught a flicker of compassion in his eyes.

'Poor you. You're going to have one hell of a bruise there by morning.' He drew back and straightened up.

'Mel!' Claire came running from the kitchen. 'What happened? Are you all right?' She bent over me with concern and glanced up at Josh for an explanation, seeing I was too dizzy to speak for myself.

'She's got a lump the size of an egg coming up on her temple,' Josh replied, frowning. 'Have you any arnica? Or witch hazel? They're both good for bruises.'

'Of course we have. We always keep a first-aid box at the ready in the bathroom. I'll run up and get some.'

* * *

Much later, swabbed, pampered by Claire and helped to bed, I lay awake staring into the darkness for a long time. It wasn't because of my injury I couldn't sleep. My mind wouldn't let me rest. It was endlessly playing over the scene with Josh Stephens, like a video re-run. What a fool I'd been, confusing him with David. Had I said anything out loud? How embarrassing if I had. Had he noticed? I would never know — he wasn't likely to mention it, was he? I just couldn't remember, and trying to do so was making my head worse.

When I eventually dozed off, it was into a slumber full of disturbing dreams. Consequently I overslept next morning. Then I found it impossible to hurry as my head still had a tendency towards dizziness, so I was forced to take my time getting ready.

'Ah, Mel, there you are.' As I reached the hall, Claire emerged from the kitchen, hastily wiping her hands on a towel. 'How are you this morning?' She peered anxiously into my face. 'What about the head?'

'Much better, thanks.' I attempted a smile, and winced. 'It's still very tender, but yes, I'm on the mend, really.'

Her expression relaxed. 'Oh, I'm so glad. We were all quite worried last night, you seemed to be so out of it.'

'I certainly was.' I recalled the dream-like sequence of events from the previous day. Now it all felt as if it had happened to somebody else. 'What a stupid thing to do. It'll teach me to watch where I'm going in future.'

'Josh was asking after you, but he had to get off to work. Two other men from his team turned up, and they went over to Wheal Hope to investigate the old workings.'

I frowned. 'Oh, I do hope they'll be careful — it's terribly dangerous over there in all those crumbling ruins.'

Claire laughed out loud as her eyes widened in disbelief. 'Mel, Josh and his team are professionals! They know the risks better than you do, they're doing this sort of work all the time. They had hard hats, steel toe-caps on their boots, ropes, torches, instruments, everything. All right?'

'Yes, yes, of course.' I bit my bottom lip. 'I just wasn't thinking straight.'

'I'll blame the bump on your head for that!' Claire chuckled and turned away.

* * *

Over the next couple of weeks we hardly saw Josh, who had taken to going out early and coming back late in

47

the evening to do little more than eat and sleep.

From what I did manage to gather, he was visiting several other old mines as well, getting background information and comparing them with Wheal Hope, in case they were connected. Geevor, which had closed fairly recently, was one of them, and the famous Crowns mine at Botallack. Here the engine houses perched part-way down the side of the cliffs, clinging on precariously just above the sea, with the workings stretching far out under the water.

During this time Easter came and went and Alex and her little girl arrived. I hadn't heard the taxi draw up and when I heard Claire calling me, I quickened my pace to see what was happening.

By the time I arrived at the entrance, Claire was helping Alex bring in what seemed to be a vast amount of luggage, followed by our little five-year-old niece, Isobel.

'Aunty Mel! Aunty Mel!' She skipped

across the courtyard, pony-tail flying. In her pink denim skirt and flowery printed top, she looked much like the pretty rag doll she carried tucked under her arm.

'Hello, sweetheart!' I swept her up in my arms. 'It's lovely to see you.'

'Mel! Hello.' Alex came across and enfolded me in a hug. I put Isobel down and returned her kiss on the cheek. Petite, vivid and impetuous, she never seemed to change. She still looked like a teenager, in jeans and a designer top, in spite of her twenty-seven years. I put it down to the active life she'd always led, from teaching PE as a career, to her love of extreme sports.

Climbing, abseiling, paragliding, white water rafting, you name it, before her marriage Alex had tried them all, travelling the world, and working at whatever came along in order to pay her way. The last trip she'd taken had involved mountaineering in Nepal. Then as she was working her way down through India before spending time in an ashram to 'recharge her batteries', she had met Andy, who'd been doing a gap year before university, and her life had changed dramatically.

'Oh, it's lovely to be here!' Alex paused on the way in to take in the view. We didn't see her very often, living just outside London as she and her husband did, and kept in touch mainly by phone.

The rest of the day flew by as she settled in and unpacked her own and Isobel's belongings.

'I'll swear this child has brought more toys and books with her than clothes!' Alex laughed, straightening up from a suitcase and running a hand through her spiky dark hair, making it stand on end more than ever.

I laughed and shrugged. 'Well, which do you think is more important when you're five years old!'

'Aunty Mel,' Isobel came bouncing into the room waving a dog lead, 'please can we take Jess for a walk? She really,

really wants to go out!'

Jess was our Border collie, a highly intelligent animal and adored by Isobel. 'How do you know she wants to?' I smiled. 'Did she say so?'

'Of course not, that's silly,' she retorted. 'I just picked up her lead and she started barking as if she was asking.'

'I see.' Suitably humbled and put in my place, I winked at Claire. 'Well, I suppose we could have a short walk before tea. Go and ask Mummy for your coat. Perhaps she'd like to come as well.'

* * *

Much later, settled in the sitting-room after a pasty supper, the three of us were relaxing at last with a cup of coffee and catching up on each other's news.

Rob was in the kitchen, reading the newspaper and listening to the radio, and Isobel was in bed, having fallen asleep almost as soon as her head touched the pillow.

'So where's Andy gone this time, did you say?' I glanced across at Alex, who had picked up a magazine which lay unopened on her lap.

'Out to the Middle East.' She shook off her moccasins and curled up in the chair. 'He's in Dubai at the moment, trying to drum up custom for the firm.'

Andy was sales rep for a computer company, and did a great deal of travelling both abroad and at home.

'Do you miss not going with him, since you had Isobel?' Claire asked.

'A bit.' Alex sighed. 'But she's worth it. I wouldn't change anything. And I'm especially glad I travelled around so much when I had the chance.'

She yawned and stretched her arms above her head. 'I think I'll have an early night, if you don't mind. It's been quite a day, and I still haven't finished unpacking my own stuff yet.'

'Of course. Sleep well.'

★   ★   ★

A few days later on an afternoon of beautiful early spring sunshine, I was setting out on my own to give Jess her daily walk. We had agreed when we first started up the business, that we should each have some time off during any week.

'Nobody works for seven days and sleeps on the job like you'll be doing.' Rob had been firm in making that rule. 'I shall be at work, so that only leaves you two and Carol to cope with everything. Of course you'll need a break.'

I was fond of Rob. Quiet and amiable on the surface, but when he made a point it was usually sensible, perceptive and forward-thinking. He was as dependable as a rock, and he and Claire rarely disagreed.

So it had been arranged that we should each have half a day a week off, in rotation. It wasn't much, but he'd been right. At the height of the season we were under huge pressure, welcome pressure in a way of course, as it meant the venture was doing really well.

But a breathing space away from it all had made a big difference to each of us and prevented the frayed tempers that sometimes threatened, from spilling over into outright rows. However, I was thinking now that Alex was here, and seemed prepared to pull her weight, perhaps we could even consider a whole day each.

Lost in these thoughts, I was startled when Josh appeared at my side as I was going through the gate.

'Do you mind if I join you for a stroll, Mel? I've been underground most of the day and I need some fresh air.'

'Of course not.' I smiled up at him, feeling my heartbeat increase a pace. It must have been the way he'd made me jump that caused it to flutter. 'I shall enjoy having some company.'

'I haven't seen you for ages, except in passing,' he remarked, closing the gate behind us. 'How's your bruise?'

'Oh, totally cleared up now. Gone

and forgotten.' I smiled up at him.

'Oh, good. You know, I felt a bit guilty about that, as if it was somehow my fault.'

'What?' I stepped back as Jess pushed past us and went hurtling off over the open country. 'How could you possibly be to blame?'

Josh shrugged and spread his hands wide. 'Because if you weren't doing me a good turn it wouldn't have happened.'

'What rubbish! You can't be serious.' I gazed at him in disbelief. 'I just wasn't looking where I was going, that's all.'

But inwardly I could feel a warm glow spreading because of his concern.

★　★　★

At first we had fallen into step, but soon the track over the moor became too narrow, and we were going in single file now, with Josh in the lead. With my gaze on the broad, muscular back in front of me, I found myself wondering about this man. Always so strong and capable in his work, until my accident I was unaware of this gentle and caring side of his character.

Josh was still leading the way as I took deep breaths of the clear, salty air and glanced over the edge as we went along. On the landward side we were about level with the clutter of loose stones and abandoned pieces of machinery that marked the fringes of Wheal Hope. I caught up with him and paused to look over the cliff.

'Did you know that small bay down there is called Kit's Cove, after a notorious local smuggler?' I pointed.

'Really?' Josh peered over with interest.

'Yes, legend has it that he kept his loot in that cave over there, which is also named after him. Kit's Cupboard.'

Josh grinned. 'Do you think there's any truth in the story?'

'Well,' I hesitated, 'of course smuggling did go on, and based on the 'no smoke without fire' idea, I'd say yes I do.' Shrugging I added, 'Not that we're ever likely to find out now. They say that the cave silted up many, many years ago.'

I smiled to myself. 'And some say old Kit still walks on Carn Dhu up there,' I pointed to the looming granite crag, 'on the darkest nights. One of those big rocks is called Kit's Chair. It's where he's supposed to sit looking through his telescope, watching for the next haul to come in.'

Josh threw back his head and laughed heartily. 'Well, maybe I'll take a walk up there one night and introduce myself to him!'

We walked companionably on round a headland where, a couple of hundred feet below us in the chasm, gulls and fulmars wheeled and screamed, their eerie cries echoing up from the depths. The sea, although benign enough today, was still pitching itself against the wicked black rocks at the bottom with a ceaseless pounding, throwing sprays of foam high into the air.

Josh glanced over his shoulder and

paused in his stride, following my gaze.

'Impressive, isn't it? Quite awesome. I've never been down here in winter but I imagine it would be pretty grim then. It was bad enough on the day Chris and I were in trouble.'

'Oh, it is.' I nodded. 'It's about the most treacherous piece of coastline there is for shipping. There have been scores of wrecks up and down here over the years. There's an inlet further up the coast that's called Hell's Mouth. For good reason.'

We walked on, past stands of low-growing gorse flaunting its brilliant gold flowers, their coconut scent wafting on the breeze. Idly I thought of the old saying, 'Kissing's out of favour when the gorse is out of bloom,' and glanced up at the tall figure beside me.

Wearing long shorts and hiking boots, his legs were lean and muscular, covered with dark hairs. There didn't seem to be an ounce of spare flesh on him.

As the wind blew, his loose sweater

flapped against his body, displaying more muscles in his broad back, rippling down his torso and tapering to a neat, narrow waist. At his open neck, more dark hairs nestled. I took a furtive glance at his left hand. He wasn't wearing a wedding ring, but then, a lot of men didn't . . .

But what was it about this man that held such fascination for me? Annoyed with myself, I whistled up the dog and strode on.

I was suddenly brought up short however as Josh, who had been humming a tune under his breath while we went, turned to me with a smile.

'Your sister Alex is an interesting person, isn't she?' He quirked an eyebrow.

Alex? Startled, I blinked and stared up at him. 'Oh, is she?'

'Yes, she was telling me about some of her adventures.' Josh put up a hand to shield his eyes from the sun. 'I used to do a lot of running myself, in my teens and early twenties, but as I became more involved with my career I had to let it lapse. I was spending a lot of time abroad then, studying different methods and gaining experience. There was never enough time for much else. Not like the long school holidays.'

'Being able to do what she loved and have a career as well, you mean. Yes, everything always turned out well for Alex. She seems to lead a charmed life.'

'And you don't?' The quiet voice took me off guard and I hardly knew how to reply.

'Oh, um, I've had my ups and downs, you know?' I kept my tone light. 'But that's all in the past now.'

Although I saw the sympathy and interest in those mesmerising eyes and was tempted to pour out the whole story, I had to tell myself that however I might feel drawn to this man, he was nevertheless a comparative stranger. And I wasn't in the habit of baring my soul to strangers.

If my voice had had an edge to it, it was because at one time I used to feel a certain amount of underlying resentment around Alex. At the way she'd always been able to avoid responsibility. Being away so much as she was, travelling the world, she was never around when she could be useful. When Dad had been taken ill it had fallen to me to leave London and my job, leave David and our life together, and give up so much in order to come down here and nurse him.

Claire had been ill herself at the time, having suffered a miscarriage with complications afterwards, so I had no choice but to take everything on to my shoulders. Alex flew home briefly for the funeral but was off again in a few days, back to somewhere in India, where she was supporting herself by teaching English and spending the rest of her time trekking and climbing in the mountains.

So by the time that was all over and Mum had been settled in her little flat, leaving the house to us, two years, nearly three had flown by, leaving my previous life in tatters. I'd lost my job, lost David, lost my friends in London and had to face the fact that a turning point had been reached.

But surprisingly, since I'd thrown myself heart and soul into this new business venture of ours, I rarely yearned for that part of my life any more, and since Alex had settled down too, all that was in the past.

I would dearly have liked to carry on talking to Josh, but just as we seemed to be having a personal conversation, I looked at my watch and realised it was past the time for me to return to the hostel.

'Oh, goodness. Josh, I have to get back! I've run over my time off. I must dash. It's my turn to help Carol cook the residents' evening meal.'

I called Jess to my side and bent to put her on the lead to break contact with Josh's deep-set dark eyes, which a moment ago had been boring into my very soul.

'Straight home and no more chasing rabbits,' I told her.

★ ★ ★

We were being kept pretty busy with visitors now that the season had started, and Alex was roped in to do her share of the work, as she'd promised. Most days she made herself useful helping Carol in the kitchen, along with Isobel, who seemed to have taken to the older woman.

Carol was a comfortable, motherly soul who had brought up several children of her own and was a doting granny of more. A widow, her grown-up children having left the nest, she had few demands on her time, and not far to come. Her cottage was within walking distance, on the winding lane between us and the rough track leading down to the sea.

She was occupying the little girl in

the kitchen today, giving her bits of cut-off pastry to play with while Carol was making pasties. As it was raining heavily, and the child could not go outside to play, the three of us breathed sighs of relief and gratitude and crept upstairs to sort out the bedrooms. Loveable as she was, we could do twice the work in half the time without Isobel's 'help'.

Alex and I started stripping beds in the men's dormitory, ready for the fresh duvet covers and pillowcases that Claire had gone to fetch.

As Claire entered the room, carrying an armful of clean bed linen, she raised her eyes to the ceiling and shrugged. 'I've just seen Isobel on her way up the stairs. She must have the attention span of a gnat, to be looking for us already.'

Alex turned from the window where she had been gazing out at the dismal landscape, partially obscured by the sheets of driving rain which were now coming down in torrents.

'Children have. And they're inquisitive little creatures. She thinks she's missing something if she can't see me and know what I'm doing. But then,' Alex gave her a bland look, 'you haven't had much experience of them, have you?'

I noticed Claire flinch and turn away, biting her lip at the tactless remark. I knew that for the last couple of years Claire and Rob had been trying for a baby, without success. Whether Alex was aware of this I wasn't sure, but if she was, then it was an unforgivable thing to say. We worked on in silence for a while.

'There, all done.' I stood back at last and surveyed with satisfaction the room with its fresh neat beds.

Especially the one in the corner. When I'd stripped that, the faint, personal scent of Josh Stephens' body rose up to me so strongly it had me rocking back on my heels in total recall. I was instantly in his arms again, my head lying on his shoulder, my hand on his heart. What a fool! I felt my cheeks flush as I relived the most embarrassing moment of my life and briskly flung open the window to let in the fresh air, damp though it was.

4

When the weather changed again after the few days when it seemed as if spring had come to stay, I wondered, as it had been relentlessly pouring down for several days, how Josh and his team were faring. They could hardly work outside in this.

I asked him one evening when I saw him drive in and park the car. He didn't seem to be very wet, and he left his jacket and the rest of his kit in the car as usual.

I held the back door open for him as he came running across the yard, holding a newspaper over his head, and stamped his feet on the mat.

'Thanks, Mel.' Josh frowned and threw himself down into a chair in the kitchen, stretching out his long legs. 'Good grief, isn't it ever going to stop raining?'

'How are you managing with your work, in all this?' I enquired, placing a mug of steaming coffee in front of him.

He took a long swig. 'Oh, that is so good. I was dying for a hot drink. You must be a mind-reader!' I felt warmth come to my cheeks, and turned away to pour one for myself.

'As for the job, I've spent a couple of days in the library up at Redruth, going through maps of the old mine workings, to see if I can find out where the adits actually were.'

'How did you get on?' I took a seat at the end of the table and rested my elbows on it.

'Not bad. I found a couple of useful leads. And when this blasted rain stops, I'm hoping to follow them up.' He ran a hand through the flop of hair on his forehead and sighed.

'You see, I'm working to a time limit, and if I get delayed too much, this job will slip through my fingers and I'll lose it entirely.' Josh spread his hands and shrugged.

'Oh? Why is that?' Genuinely interested, I kept the conversation going. It was one of very few conversations we'd had, apart from pleasantries, and I wanted to find out more about this disturbing man.

I was angry with myself for the way he was getting under my skin, but Josh seemed to be subconsciously lodged at the back of my mind as a permanent presence, however much I tried to forget him.

I suppose it wasn't his fault that he was able to exert such a hold on me; it was mine. Josh had never treated me any differently from the rest of the family, nor given the slightest hint that I was any more to him than an acquaintance. And I had sworn never to be swayed by a man again. Although I knew I was feeling bereft of what amounted to basic human contact. Like a warm hand in mine, a sympathetic squeeze of a shoulder, an impulsive hug . . . Just little reassuring things I used to take so much for granted.

'It's like this, Mel.' Josh drummed his fingers on the table-top and jerked me out of my self-absorption. 'My employers have enough money in the can to reopen a mine, right?'

I nodded and frowned, trying to concentrate.

'One mine,' Josh emphasised, giving a glum look at the sheets of rain cascading down the window.

'Well, being a Cornishman, of course I want this job to come to Cornwall. Goodness knows the county needs it badly enough. Needs all the money and employment opportunities it can get, you know?'

'I do. You're absolutely right. Especially in this area.'

'But, it's a toss-up between our Wheal Hope out there,' Josh jerked his head towards the window, 'and another one they've got their sights on, in Mexico. They've got men out there looking over that one, just as we're doing down here. Whichever is the more viable proposition, they'll go for.'

He paused thoughtfully and swirled his remaining coffee round and round the mug. 'And there's something else.' He raised his head and our glances met. 'Mel, if I can secure this contract for my firm, I'll be in with a chance of promotion.' His expression hardened. 'At thirty I guess it's about time I moved up the scale.'

Thirty. So he was only two years older than me. Although why this information should matter, defeated me.

'Oh, I see.' My face cleared. 'Now I can understand the pressure you're working under.'

'Too true. And the weather is not helping us one bit.' He banged down a fist, making the coffee-mug jump. Then placing his arms behind his head he leaned back, tipping the chair on two legs, and added with the ghost of a grin, 'And I bet it's not raining in Mexico!'

With this lightening of Josh's previous and more serious mood, I decided to make the most of the moment and

71

do a bit of unashamed fishing into his private life, about which I knew nothing at all.

Rising, I picked up the empty mugs and strolled across to put them in the sink, keeping my tone of voice light and casual. 'Which part of Cornwall do you come from, Josh?'

'Oh, originally from St Austell. My father was a chemist, he worked in the lab of a china-clay firm. But I live in Saltash now. Which is too far to commute down here every day.'

Josh smiled but did not elaborate, and although I hadn't learned very much, I could hardly ask any more direct questions. Besides he was getting to his feet, ready to leave the room.

'Well, I must get back to where I belong,' he laughed. 'In the residents' quarters.'

'Oh, no,' I hurried to reassure him, 'it's quite all right. You're very welcome to join us whenever you like. With a long-term stay like yours, circumstances are a bit different from those of the weekly or two-weekly boarders.'

'Thanks, Mel, I appreciate it.' He smiled. 'Right now though,' he indicated the laptop he'd brought in with him, 'I have work to do.'

★ ★ ★

I didn't see much of Josh for a few days after that. He was away a lot at the site, going out early and only coming back for the evening meal, after which he would disappear up to his bedroom to work.

I was kept busy with the business and minor domestic problems. Like the day when the industrial-size washing machine we kept in a former 'privy' outside the back door, decided to flood all over the floor. We usually did the laundry overnight, to take advantage of the cheaper rate, so by the time the problem was discovered not only was the room awash, but there was a tide coming down the path and seeping in through the kitchen door.

It took us a whole day to mop up and dry out, get a plumber to call, and eventually finish the laundry.

As luck would have it, the weather was still against us, still damp and nasty with a seeping fog drifted in from the sea, obscuring the landscape in a woolly grey cloud. So instead of hanging it all outside to blow as we usually did, we were forced to use the tumble drier, creating more expense we could well have done without.

* * *

So after all that, I was delighted to get a phone call from Samantha, a friend of mine from my nursing days. A city girl through and through, she had been good to me when I was going through my bad patch. Good for me too, in that her cheery, outgoing nature and practical attitude to problems shook me out of my tendency to over-sensitivity.

'Forget him, Mel,' she'd said breezily, when I'd told her about David. 'Who needs men?' She was whisking me out to lunch as she spoke. 'Love them and leave them, I say. There are plenty more pebbles on the beach, you know.'

Now I smiled at the recollection as I heard her voice on the phone. 'I've got a few days leave . . . staying in a B&B in Penzance. Ben's going off fishing all day . . . how about us going to a matinee at the Minack? Lunch and a catch-up first? Can you take that much time off from your particular grindstone?'

I chuckled as we made a firm arrangement and hung up. So Ben must be her latest pebble on the beach. Last time we spoke it had been Nathan. Love them and leave them . . . Well, it was a point of view, I suppose.

Lost in my own thoughts, I wandered back to the sitting-room and had just closed the door behind me and sat down, when Josh knocked and pushed it open again.

'Sorry to bother you, Mel, but I wonder if I could possibly store something in your office for a short time? It won't take up much room, but it's quite important and I don't want to leave it in my room, or the residents' lounge.'

We had been sitting round the table, Alex, Claire and I, playing Ludo with Isobel, who was bored at being kept indoors by the rain. It was an old set left over from our own childhood, which had somehow survived being thrown out long ago, and she was captivated by it.

At the sight of that disarming smile however and the familiar unruly flop of hair, my treacherous heartbeat quickened, as I jumped to my feet again and crossed the room towards him.

'Yes, of course you can. Come and see where would be the best place for it.'

'I'm sorry to intrude on your private space,' he said, following me down the passage, 'but I couldn't think of any alternative.' He stood to one side as I gathered up the papers I'd been working on earlier and shelved them.

'No, no, not at all. How much space do you need?'

'It's just this box-file of photos.' Josh knelt down and pulled it out of a rucksack he'd dumped on the floor. As the lid of the file sprang open he indicated the contents and spread his hands in explanation.

'We have to be so meticulous in this job, you see. We've spent so many hours climbing around caves where old remains can still be seen, and studying cliff faces, that I can't risk precious records like this getting lost. Although I've backed them up on a memory stick as well, I'm a belt and braces man by nature.' He chuckled.

'What is this a picture of?' I asked ungrammatically, peering closer at what looked like a black hole in some rock.

Josh sat back on his heels. 'Well, to understand properly, I shall have to give you a lesson in geophysical surveying techniques. It's not as dry as it sounds,' he added hastily, smiling as he must have seen the look on my face.

'Abandoned underground workings are terribly risky to anyone thinking of opening them up.' Josh counted on his fingers. 'One, in most cases, water has accumulated and the lower levels are flooded. Two, poisonous gases may be present. Three, old supports may have rusted or rotted and can collapse beneath the weight of any machinery on the surface.'

'Oh, I see what you mean. I've never thought of all that before,' I admitted.

'No reason why you should.' Josh laughed. 'Anyway, that's the reason we do a careful survey from the top and map out as much as we can before going in.'

It was very quiet in the tiny room. Rob had converted it from the old pantry adjoining the kitchen, and there was little more in it than a computer desk, a chair and a few wall shelves. Nobody came in here apart from me, or rarely did, as I was the one who did the administration and office work relating to the business.

Now however it seemed crowded and rather warm, as I became very conscious of Josh's proximity.

Kneeling at my feet as he was, from this angle I could see there were actually little bronze-coloured highlights in his hair, which I'd thought up to now was black. My hand, as if it had a will of its own, was itching to reach out and stroke back the flop over his forehead which seemed to always fall that way . . . I jerked back to reality as he spoke, and thrust the hand into my jeans pocket.

'Anyway,' Josh turned back to the box in front of him. 'As for the photo, it's a picture of an old adit coming out of a cliff face, from a different mine. It's not far from Wheal Hope, and I did think they were connected, but no, there should be another one.' He spread his hands in frustration. 'We need to find that, and soon, so we can tell where the bottom level will be. Then we can start work properly.'

'And you're racing against time, you

said, didn't you?'

Josh nodded and glanced up at the shelves. 'Yes, that's about the size of it.'

He raised his eyebrows.

'So, have you got a bit of shelf space you could spare for the file, Mel? I can see how cramped for room you are in here, but I'd be really grateful.'

'Oh, yes, of course.' I turned away and reached up to the top shelf. 'I'll just push this stuff up a bit.' I moved along some folders and made a space at the end. It'll be quite safe there.'

'Oh, thanks. That's great.' He took a small step forward.

However, I'd put one foot on the bottom shelf to help me reach up, and as I came down I stumbled and automatically grabbed at Josh's arm, it being the nearest thing to me, to steady my balance.

At that moment I heard a piping voice calling my name, followed by thumping feet coming down the passage, and Isobel poked her small, cross face round the door.

'Come on, Aunty Mel, it's your turn. We can't play any more until you come back. What are you doing in here?'

Josh had instinctively put an arm around my waist as I staggered and now I saw how we must look to the child's eyes, seemingly locked in a clinch.

I felt my face flame and jumped quickly away, making me I suppose, appear even more flustered to Isobel, who had fixed us with a round, calculating stare of her dark eyes.

'Storing away some precious secret treasure of mine where it'll be safe,' Josh said jokingly, raising a hand and playfully ruffling her hair. 'Cheer up, munchkin, we're all done now. Sorry I interrupted your game.'

Isobel's eyes widened even more. 'Precious treasure? Like gold and jewels, you mean? Can I see? Please?' She stood on tiptoe and craned her neck towards the top shelf.

'No, no, nothing like that at all.' Josh laughed as her face fell. 'I was only teasing. It's just boring old work stuff.

Not precious to anybody but me.' He picked up his rucksack. 'So there we are. You can have Mel back now.'

Isobel didn't move away immediately but stood solemnly regarding us. 'Carol says there's real treasure hidden in a cave down on the beach.' Her eyes widened. 'Smuggler's treasure. Can we go and look when it stops raining?'

I smiled at the earnest little face. 'Oh, Izzy, that's only a very old story. It's not really true. Do you know what a legend is?'

As the child shook her head, Josh crouched down to her level. 'It's like a fairy story, that's all. Like Goldilocks and Red Riding Hood — you know they're not real, don't you?'

Isobel slowly nodded, then scowled at us both and stomped off down the corridor towards the sitting-room. I smiled and raised an eyebrow to Josh as I meekly followed in her wake.

★ ★ ★

By next morning the rain had at last blown over and the sun that was shining actually had some warmth in it. The sea was reflecting the bright blue of the arching sky and everywhere was looking well-washed and sparkling.

Lured outside by the sunshine, Claire and I with mugs of coffee in our hands, had wandered over to the picnic table that stood on a patch of rough grass at the front of the house. It sloped down to a wood paling fence, where Mum when she had been able, had made a border of hardy plants. Some of the bushier shrubs still survived, struggling against the salt-laden Atlantic gales. There was rosemary, a tall, feathery tamarisk and some escallonia covered in bright pink flowers.

Beyond the fence marking the boundary of our property lay the wilderness of open moorland. Scrubby heather and low-growing gorse dotted with huge boulders tumbled towards the sea, which today was playfully winking its sapphire eye at us.

It was very peaceful where we were, and we'd been idly chatting about all the tasks that needed to be done that day.

'Well, I suppose we'd better get on with it then, hadn't we?' I stretched my arms lazily above my head. 'Sitting out here talking won't get us anywhere.'

I laughed and drained the last of my drink. I was just rising to my feet when Isobel came marching purposefully past us with a tin bowl of dog food in one hand and her doll in the other.

'I'm going to give Jess her breakfast,' she announced and set it down outside the kennel. As she turned back, Josh came around the corner of the house, on his way to work and she skipped over to him, thrusting a hand into his and chattering animatedly as he made his way towards the car.

'Isobel's quite taken with Josh,' Claire remarked. 'He seems to have a natural way with children.'

'Perhaps he has some of his own.' I shrugged. 'I know nothing of his personal circumstances. Do you?'

Claire shook her head and we fell silent as they approached.

Isobel was staring at us now with a calculating gleam, and I wondered what was going on in that small, neat head of hers. However, it wasn't long before I found out when she wrapped both arms tightly round the doll and held it up to her face.

'I saw Josh hugging Aunty Mel like this,' she said, putting her head on one side and looking up at Claire. 'In the office. When they didn't know I was there.' She stuck her button nose in the air and smirked. 'He looked like he was going to kiss her.' She fell silent, waiting for our reaction.

I immediately felt my face flame and knew I was looking as guilty as if there really had been something going on between us. I glanced at Josh who frowned and glowered at the child.

'Your imagination is too lively for your own good, young lady.' He pointed a finger at her. 'Mel tripped over and I caught her so she wouldn't fall. Like this.'

He moved to my side and nudged me so that I stumbled and he wrapped his arms around me in a clinch. Then scowling, he brought our two faces so close we were almost touching.

'And this.' His arm tightened and his cheek met mine. 'And that was all. OK?'

★ ★ ★

But it wasn't all to me. And to Josh? It was hard to tell. As our skin came into contact and he turned his head towards me, I was very aware of the flame that leapt between us. But was he? Did I imagine that his eyes softened as they met mine? Or that he held me to him a fraction longer than was strictly necessary before gently withdrawing his arm?

But as Isobel cowered away and buried her face in the doll's hair, I think I was the only one to notice the stranger who was approaching round the corner of the house, and who must have witnessed the whole little scene.

A split second later I recognised him. Then I gasped as I felt all the colour drain from my face.

5

A tall man with a shock of fair hair was standing coolly regarding us, his hands thrust into the trouser pockets of his neat grey suit. As he rocked back on his heels, appraising us with cool, blue eyes, I felt my jaw drop.

I froze, my stomach knotted and my heart began to hammer painfully against my ribs. For I had never expected to see him again, ever.

* * *

'David!' I felt all the colour from my face come flooding back in a tide of heat as I realised what he must think we were doing. I jumped away from Josh as if scalded, and stood with trembling legs, transfixed.

'Hello, Mel.' David advanced towards me as he spoke, spread his arms wide and enveloped me in a hug, then firmly kissed me on the cheek. I wriggled uncomfortably then pulled away, very conscious of Josh's presence and his raised eyebrows in the background. I had to restrain myself from rubbing a hand over my face as if David had violated it.

I was dimly aware of Isobel's piping voice as well. 'Who's that man, Aunty Claire? Why is he kissing Aunty Mel? Does he love her?' I cringed even more.

Claire murmured some reply and took the child's hand to lead her away, Isobel staring over her shoulder as she went.

'What are you d-doing here?' I stammered, still in a state of utter shock.

'Looking for you.' His steady gaze was raking me up and down. 'Is there somewhere we can talk?' He pointedly turned his back on Josh and the others. 'Privately?'

'Oh, um, yes, of course.' I forcibly pulled myself together. 'Come inside.'

I led the way into our private sitting-room and closed the door behind us. David strolled over and glanced out of the window before sitting down beside me on the large, comfy sofa.

'Nice place you've got here, Mel. Lovely position, too. I had a look around, as there was no-one in reception.' He raised an eyebrow and the corners of his mouth lifted.

I immediately took this to be a veiled rebuke. He was hinting that I'd abandoned my post. And where had I been instead . . . ? I raised my chin and looked him full in the face.

The face that had once been as familiar to me as my own. It hadn't changed. That little brown mole on his temple — I'd kissed it a hundred times. I knew the dimple on one side of his mouth, and the way his eyes crinkled at the corners when he laughed. I'd worshipped this face once, with all the passion of young love.

But that was then. This was also the

man who had shown no compassion or finer feelings when I had been torn between that love, and duty to my needy and dependent parents. I stared impassively at him.

'Yes, it is. And you could have rung the service bell.' I took a deep breath. 'But I don't suppose you've come to talk about the view, have you?' I said, still staring him down. 'So, what do you want, David?'

He averted his eyes and was looking down at his lap now, where his long, clever fingers played nervously with the ends of his tie.

David? Nervous? I almost laughed out loud. This was 'Dr David', the man who strode about the hospital in his white coat, a god-like figure larger than life, his slightest word law.

I glanced at the wavy, blond head at my side. Recalling how I used to run my fingers through that shining mop, and wondering why I didn't feel like doing so now.

I caught a whiff of aftershave and for

a second I was transported back to Josh's arms, that very same fragrance wafting over me. I'd lain there then, thinking of this man and all he had meant to me — once.

Not any more, though. Once, I'd been a naïve young girl who had known nothing of life, and to me at that time, he was as remote and as intimidating as a god. All the young nurses went weak at the knees at the sight of him and I, whose self-esteem had been next to nil, had been so overwhelmed that this gorgeous creature could actually condescend to take an interest in me, that I was putty in his hands.

I'd thought I was in love, of course. And I had loved him, with all the fervour and pain of the young. He was the first man I'd known intimately, and during our relationship I had grown from a girl into an adult woman. The callow youngsters, almost as naïve as myself, who were all I'd known up until then, had paled into insignificance beside him. And here he was, raising wary eyes to mine as he took in a deep breath.

'Mel, I've realised what a big mistake I made by letting you go.' A pulse beat in his temple and colour rose to his cheeks as he reached for my hand. When I withdrew it and glared fiercely at him, he jerked back as if shot.

I wasn't going to help him out, or make it easy. Let him squirm for a bit, why not? So I stayed silent as he stumbled on, thinking, with some satisfaction I must admit, how much this must be costing him in self-esteem. To come all this way to apologise, as he seemed to be doing, must have been a struggle for such an arrogant man.

I glanced at the perfect profile as he withdrew eye contact for a moment. There was the spotless shirt, the Raybans tucked into his breast pocket. David never 'did' casual. Whatever the occasion he was always impeccably groomed, not a hair out of place. Nothing had changed there, then.

I'd never seen him in a pair of jeans

all the time we lived together. I used to admire this in him, but now I found it slightly irritating that a man could spend so much time cultivating his own image.

'I've never felt for any woman since, the way I felt — and still feel — about you.' The soft, persuasive voice failed to move me. On the contrary.

So, there had been others then, plural, over the intervening years. But of course there had. I recalled the entourage of nurses both young and not so young, who had all been only too ready to fall at his expensively-shod feet, given half a chance.

'I tried to forget you and bury all the old memories in work, endless work. But my life suddenly seemed so empty.' David shrugged then clasped his hands together. 'I kept seeing you bustling about the wards, your earnest, pointed little face, your soothing voice. So conscientious, so caring.'

He reached for my hand again, but I folded my arms and pretended I hadn't noticed. 'And when we were in bed together too,' he went on smoothly, 'you were so warm, so giving . . . Mel, I miss you so much.' His voice trailed away.

I'd missed that side of our relationship as well, to begin with. But now I'd become so used to sleeping alone with only my thoughts to keep me company, I'd almost forgotten what it felt like to share.

Suddenly David rose to his feet and began to pace up and down. 'And I threw it all away because my stupid pride got in the way.' He struck his palm with a fist. Rather theatrical, I thought. But David always had enjoyed playing to an audience.

'Because I couldn't bear to accept the fact that you didn't put me first. Mel, I was so selfish! Of course you had to come and look after your parents. And I didn't even try to put myself in your position, to realise what a sacrifice you were making — your career, your prospects, everything you'd worked for.'

Deflated by this outburst, David

stopped in his tracks and thrust his hands into his pockets as he gazed hopefully at me.

'And you?' His voice dropped to little more than a whisper. 'I know it's a lot to expect, but how would you feel about us getting together again?'

I lifted my shoulders in a huge sigh of nostalgia, for my life could have been so different. But better? I rose to my feet as well, and restlessly moved about the room. Through the window I caught a glimpse of Josh, deep in conversation with one of his team-mates who had just come in.

Josh was standing facing him, earnestly making a point and gesticulating with one hand. I studied his vivid, mobile face, white teeth gleaming in that familiar grin, the unruly hair tossing in the wind, and my heart turned over. There was such a vibrancy about him, a charisma I could feel even from here. Something that was totally lacking in the man at my side.

So, would it have been a better life

with David? No. Not in a million years.

David had his good points of course. He was a wonderful doctor, highly thought of in his profession. On a personal level however, he was the sort of man who would never take the slightest risk, in case something went wrong. Totally conventional, a little old-fashioned, predictable and just plain dull, he would make some woman a good, steady husband. However, that woman would not be me.

He must have been following my sight-line out of the window.

'But there's someone else, isn't there?' he added.

I wouldn't give him the satisfaction of admitting or denying that one. Ignoring the question, I turned back into the room and tilting my chin, met that probing gaze head on.

'David,' I stared impassively back at him. 'You must understand how time has moved on. I'm not the same person as I was when we were together. I was young, inexperienced — '

'So you're telling me that you're now experienced?' His lip curled in anger and he glanced away. 'But of course . . . that chap out there, the one who was all over you when I arrived, it's him, isn't it?'

I ignored that remark too, but Josh's face and heart-stopping smile swam before my eyes. The sudden stark contrast between the two men proved to me, if I needed proof, where my heart truly lay. Unlikely as it was that anything would come out of it. But my future certainly did not lie with this man.

I took a deep breath and ploughed on. 'Oh, this is so hard to explain. David, I realise now that what I felt for you then was pure passion. You aroused feelings in me I'd never had before.' I spread my hands and willed him to see the position from my point of view. I remembered it was something he'd never been very good at.

'I was so naïve, I mistook my feelings for love.' I lifted my chin. 'You seemed so sure of yourself, so confident, so worldly, all the things I wasn't. It's taken me all these years to see clearly the way it actually was.'

I gazed steadily into his stormy eyes. 'I've made a life for myself since then, a satisfying life, even if I am still single.' I paused, then took a deep breath. 'And David, that is why I have to tell you, my answer is no.'

'B — but, Mel . . . ' He was looking completely shell-shocked, as if this was the last thing he'd expected. 'I can give you a much better life than you have here!'

He spread his arms wide. 'I'm not badly off now I've climbed a bit further up the ladder. You wouldn't need to go out to work at all.' He was still gazing at me in astonishment.

'I came down here intending to ask you to marry me, Mel.' His tone had changed to a pleading and unpleasant whine. 'You're the only woman I've ever felt that way about.' He took a step closer and held out both hands to me.

'We could have a nice home, do a bit of entertaining, maybe in future have a . . . a family.' He finished abruptly as he must have seen the fury in my face.

Incensed, I stamped a foot as I tried to get through to him. 'But can't you see that I like the work I'm doing here, that it gives me fulfilment and satisfaction? That I don't want to be a housewife in your home, entertaining your friends! David, we shall never see eye to eye about this, we are poles apart, and that's the way we shall remain. Apart.' As I raised my furious face to his, I saw his eyes widen in shock at my icy reply.

'You've got a nerve, David Lang!' I clasped my arms about myself as I paced the room. 'Get together again? Do you honestly think you can just breeze in here after what . . . five years without a word, and expect me to welcome you back with open arms? Just pick up where we left off?' With a hollow laugh I turned on a heel.

'You must be joking! And can you

imagine what a shock this has been for me?' I turned to face him again. 'I spent all that time trying to forget you, and thought I'd succeeded . . . then suddenly here you are — a ghost from the past.'

He nodded, his intense gaze never wavering. 'Of course I do. And I'm sorry it had to be like this, Mel.' He scuffed a foot in the carpet. 'But I was afraid if I contacted you first, you would refuse to see me at all.'

I tightened my arms around my body as he came to a standstill facing me and raised pleading eyes to mine. Years ago that look would have reduced me to a quivering jelly, but not any more. It had no effect on me whatsoever. I could have been dead inside for all that I felt for this man now.

I took in a deep breath. 'To say I was heartbroken at the way you treated me, is a cliché, but that's exactly what it felt like at the time. My mind was in turmoil, trying to work out what to do for the best. I was worried sick about my father's illness, anxious as to how Mum was coping, stressed out by trying to be in two places at once.'

I glared steadily at him and he broke the eye contact, lowering his head to look down at the floor. 'And when I needed your support, advice and sympathy, you just weren't there.'

Now when he raised his head again, his eyes were blazing with anger. 'And I don't suppose for a moment you tried to put yourself in my place, did you? I was going through one hell of a time myself then, working punishing hours, not getting enough sleep. Trying to save lives for goodness sake. You didn't have the monopoly on stress, you know.'

'Oh, I remember all right,' I replied through gritted teeth. 'You were 'Dr. David' — all efficiency and bombast. Then coming home to me to have your ego boosted by your willing slave!'

It was no exaggeration. David, having been brought up by a widowed mother who had doted on him, had expected me to fit her image. To keep house, prepare meals, iron his shirts and warm his bed, like a dutiful wife.

Only I wasn't his wife. I worked as many hours as he did and held down a demanding job too. The memories still rankled, and I could have kicked myself for not seeing the truth long ago.

I gazed at him with scorn. 'But it's far too late to change things now, David. I've got a good life here and people who depend on me.'

He took a step forward and urgently seized my hand. 'It's never too late to make amends, if you're willing. Mel, tell me you'll think about it.'

Pulling away, I crossed to the window and looked out at the familiar scene. How hard we had all worked to bring this dream to fruition. It had been the best therapy I could have had at the time. When I had been grieving and trying to come to terms with all I'd lost, it had given me direction. And solace.

'How long are you down here for?' I asked dully.

'For about a fortnight, Mel. I'm

working as a locum in Penzance and living in the hospital,' he replied to my back.

Then I saw red. Seething, I whirled round to face him. 'So you didn't drive over three hundred miles down here just to see me at all! I was just a secondary consideration, was I? You thought it would be useful to look up little Mel. To pass the time when you weren't working!'

I looked him scornfully up and down. 'In fact that's all I ever was to you. Useful. I can see it so plainly now. David, I gave you everything I had in me, keeping nothing back. And you used me, because it was convenient to do so. Our relationship was never anything but one big lie!'

And realising this, I was surprised it didn't hurt at all. Where I should have expected to feel grief stricken, or bitter, there was nothing. In fact, what I actually felt was relief.

Because I was free at last. This meeting was the final closure of that episode in my life, and my spirits lifted. I smiled inwardly. I ought to be grateful in a way to David for showing up. For if he hadn't done, I might have always wondered how things might have been.

Now as he stood dumbstruck and wide-eyed, I knew I was right. 'You are despicable, David Lang!' I stamped a foot. 'Now get out of here! I never want to see you again.'

I turned my back as I swallowed down my fury. And when I looked round again he was nowhere to be seen.

* * *

'Are you all right, Mel?' Alex's voice jerked me out of my thoughts. 'I just passed your visitor, striding out to his car with such a furious look on his face I don't think he even saw me.'

I'd been choking back tears, of rage mostly, certainly not grief. Rage that he'd managed to churn me up into such a state, just when I thought my life was so ordered and peaceful.

Alex was looking at me with concern. Seeing my stricken face, she put an arm around my shoulder. 'Claire told me who he was. What did he say to upset you so?'

'I'm not really upset,' I sniffed. 'It was just so unexpected.' I gave her a watery smile. 'Sit down and I'll tell you all about it.'

6

Back at my desk in reception a little later, I was still shaken and finding it hard to concentrate on the register in front of me. I was supposed to be checking what change-over in guests we were expecting this coming weekend, and making sure a room was kept free for Josh to move into.

I was vaguely aware of the front door opening, but lost in thought, I didn't raise my head. When a sudden male voice jerked me out of my reverie, I looked up and there was Josh leaning his forearms on the desk, regarding me with a twinkle in his eyes.

'Penny for them,' he said with a wide smile.

'Oh, Josh! Sorry, I was miles away.' I ran a hand through my hair and gave him my full attention.

'I could see that, and I won't

interrupt your work for more than a minute. I just wanted to ask you something.'

I raised my brows and waited as he drummed his fingers on the desk and cleared his throat. 'The fact is, um, Mel, I don't know your taste in entertainment, but there's a concert on in Truro one Saturday later this month, and I'm thinking of going. It's a programme of light classical music — cheerful stuff that everybody knows.' He straightened and looked into my face. 'And I was wondering . . . whether you'd like to come. If you can spare the time that is.'

Would I! Wild horses wouldn't keep me away. The fact that I hadn't been out anywhere for ages was reason enough, but a whole carefree evening spent with Josh . . . my heartbeat quickened.

'I'd love to, Josh. Thank you.' Nothing in my restrained reply betrayed my racing pulse or the fluttering of excitement deep inside me.

But an underlying little niggle of worry was hovering at the back of my mind. 'When exactly is it, though?'

He told me the date.

My heart plummeted. That was the very day I'd arranged to meet Sam and not matter what, I couldn't let her down.

'Oh, no!' I wailed, clapping one hand to my mouth. 'That's the only day I can't go!' Wide-eyed, I tried to explain.

'Oh, Josh, I'm so sorry, but an old friend of mine from London has asked me to go out then. We've already made an arrangement for that Saturday night.'

Josh's smile suddenly vanished and now he was regarding me with a face like thunder. 'Oh. I see,' he said briefly and turned on a heel. 'Well, that's that, then.'

I rose to my feet and spread my hands in frustration. How could I make him understand how I would have given anything to go with him instead? Of course, there was no way I could.

'We've booked to go to the Minack,' I said. 'You know, the outdoor theatre on the cliffs at Porthcurno?'

Why was he so annoyed? It was just one of those things. Disappointment and hurt seared through me like a knife. Maybe Josh would suggest another occasion.

But he just gave a curt nod. 'I know it,' he grunted and began to walk away. And that was all. He was leaving the room. What had I said? It was nobody's fault, just an unfortunate coincidence.

'Perhaps another time, Josh,' I called after him. He half-turned and hunched a shoulder.

'Yes, maybe.' His footsteps echoed down the passage as I sat there dumbfounded.

I nearly burst into stupid tears again. I'd been feeling fragile enough before this, but now the added frustration was making my head spin. I felt like banging it on the desk in front of me and wailing like a child.

* * *

I couldn't relax properly for the rest of that day. That night I found myself lying awake for hours, unable to settle, unable to switch off my busy brain. The more I told myself to unwind, get some sleep, for we had another hectic day tomorrow, the more restless I became.

After tossing and turning for a while longer, I was no nearer to falling asleep than when I had come to bed. The air was close and the room felt stuffy although the window was wide open. My throat felt dry as chalk and I wished I'd brought a glass of water up with me.

Sighing, I swung my legs out of bed and thrust my feet into slippers. I would creep downstairs and make myself a cup of tea. Then try again to get some rest. I swung my dressing gown round my shoulders and tiptoed from the room.

It was equally stuffy in the kitchen, where the last of the day's heat was still trapped, along with the lingering warmth from Carol's last baking session. I certainly didn't need my robe on. Impatiently I shrugged it off and tossed it over a chair as I switched on the little spotlight over the worktop. I reached for the kettle and a mug.

I'd taken some milk from the fridge and was just turning back into the room with my tea, when I heard a strange noise. A shuffling sound, like stealthy footsteps in the passage outside.

I froze, my heart in my mouth as I whirled round and looked towards the door. Framed in the opening, for I hadn't bothered to close it, was a tall, dark, faceless figure.

An intruder? A ghost? An illusion — just a trick of the light? All the fantasies that come to haunt the mind in the middle of the night shot through my head in a moment of sheer, primeval terror.

I screamed and recoiled, my hand shook, and hot tea splashed all over the floor, down the front of my nightshirt and over my slippered feet. I screamed again and backed up against the fridge in panic as the figure advanced into the room.

'Mel!'

'Josh!'

For a split second we stood transfixed, staring at each other in astonishment.

'How dare you creep up on me in the dark like that!' I yelled, trembling with shock. 'Look what you've done!'

'Oh my god, are you scalded?' Josh jerked into action. Grabbing a tea towel in one hand and my elbow with the other, he pushed me into a chair. Pulling off my sodden slippers he gently dabbed at my feet, then my hands and arms.

'Does that hurt?' He looked anxiously into my face.

I shook my head. 'Luckily I take a lot of milk in my tea. It was hot, but not enough to burn.' I lifted my shaking arms as he started wiping at the splashes on my nightshirt. 'But you gave me such a fright! You idiot. What were you doing, creeping around in the dark on this side of the house?'

'Simple.' His hand slowed and he glanced up at me. 'I saw the light and wondered if there was an intruder, or whether it had been left on by accident.'

'And I thought you were the intruder!' Our glances met and I glowered at him. Through the haze of shock, I noticed he had bare feet and was clad in a half-length towelling robe. My subconscious mind wondered what, if anything, he was wearing underneath it . . .

'I should have realised that an intruder probably wouldn't have switched on the light, but at the time I didn't think.' Josh sat back on his heels, looking contrite. 'I'm so sorry I made you jump like that, Mel.'

'I should think so too.' I gulped and my voice wobbled. Now the initial shock was waning, I was close to tears.

'Just look at the mess I'm in!' I wailed, opening my hands as I glanced down at my ruined nightshirt.

My eyes were suddenly transfixed with horror. Where the thin cotton had been wetted, it was now practically transparent. And Josh's touch was rapidly doing things to my body I hardly dared think about.

I swallowed hard. 'My ... my dressing gown ... over there. Please.' I pointed.

Josh passed it to me and held it open while I slipped my arms into it and pulled it tightly round me. He did not however, remove his hand from my shoulder immediately, but slipped into the chair next to mine and eyed me with concern.

'Are you sure you're all right, Mel?' The melting eyes were gazing intently into mine, and trapped by their magnetism, I couldn't drag my own away. I could feel the warmth of his hand through the fabric of my robe and I couldn't move. I wanted this blissful moment to last forever, just Josh and me, cocooned in the warmth and darkness of the night.

I nodded. 'Yes, truly,' I whispered. In the half-light Josh's eyes were huge and mysterious. I wondered what he was thinking. He seemed in no more of a hurry to move than I was.

Sitting as close together as we were, I could see a little tuft of his dark hair sticking up straight from the rest, almost touching my cheek, and I had to physically restrain myself from reaching out to smooth it flat. As my head crept nearer and nearer to his shoulder I raised my face to look into his, and holding my breath, waited for what must surely come . . .

'That's OK, then.' Josh shifted his hand and moved away. I jumped like a frightened rabbit and straightened up, the illusion of closeness shattered in a second. But there was no way I'd let him see how vulnerable I'd been.

'I must get cleaned up.' I rose abruptly to my feet. 'I couldn't get to sleep before this happened,' I snapped at him, 'and now it's even less likely — thanks to you.'

I held my head high and tried to preserve my dignity as I crossed the room.

But Josh reached out an arm like steel and grabbed my wrist, whirling me round to face him. All the former warmth had ebbed from his eyes, leaving them like black pebbles.

'So you're saying it was my fault?' He glared, pinning my arm behind me. 'For goodness sake, woman, it was a simple accident. Yes, I made you jump, but it was with the best of intentions.'

I tried to wriggle out of his grasp, but he was too strong. 'Think about it, Miss High And Mighty Treloar,' he hissed. 'I didn't have to get out of my warm bed to come and investigate the sound I heard in your quarters. I could have turned over, ignored it and let the phantom burglar get away with whatever he fancied. And next time that's exactly what I shall do!'

I glared at him and swallowed hard, searching my brain for some cutting rejoinder, but none came. Then, lost for a quick retort, and unable to share with him my deepest feelings, frustration suddenly boiled up in me, red and furious. I brought my free hand up to his face and slapped it soundly.

Josh recoiled in astonishment, released me and covered his cheek with a hand.

His face like thunder, he took a step back, his eyes boring into mine. 'I didn't deserve that!'

He didn't. Of course he didn't. It was only my pent-up emotions boiling over. Oh, if only I could explain.

'I . . . I . . . ' All the fight went out of me and my shoulders slumped. As I left the room I could see a red weal already showing on his cheek as Josh removed his hand and turned his back on me.

Dismally I crept upstairs, ripped off my soiled nightshirt and crawled under the duvet. I never wanted to come out again.

Of course I still couldn't sleep. I was even more disturbed than before. A re-run of the scene with Josh in the kitchen continued to play behind my eyes on a loop, in all its full horror.

How could I have been so horrible to him? To the man I loved most of all in the world. For yes, I was forced to acknowledge it at last. In the depth of the night I could no longer delude myself. I loved Josh Stephens with all my heart and soul. That he didn't feel the same way about me made no difference to that.

I did weep then. In the darkness and silence I wept for all that might have been, for my shattered dreams, and for the lonely future I saw looming ahead of me.

Worse still, I would have to face Josh in the morning and apologise, wouldn't I?

* * *

Having been able to snatch no more than two or three hours of fitful sleep, I staggered out of bed early next morning, showered and dressed before anyone was about, and crept blearily downstairs.

I leaned my hot forehead on the cool glass of the windowpane and looked out across the moor. Dawn was just breaking over the sea, where a bank of pearl-grey cloud was parting to reveal streaks of pink and primrose light. I stood transfixed by the beauty of the morning. It was magical. Somewhere nearby a drowsy bird was tuning up, and drops of dew on the sparse grass of the garden were beginning to twinkle with a myriad jewel-like colours.

I stepped outdoors and walked to the end of the garden. A brilliant tapestry of interwoven heather and gorse in regal shades of purple and gold stretched across the moor as far as the sea. There was hardly enough breeze to stir their fragrance, but diligent bees were already at work among the flowers. I took a deep breath of the reviving air and felt better, resolving to do this more often.

However, as I turned to go back, I heard the side door of the house slam and caught a glimpse of Josh hurrying round the corner towards his car. My heart lurched and my mouth dried up. This had to be the moment. If I put it off now I would never do it. I scurried across the grass and softly called his name.

I saw his back stiffen, then slowly Josh turned round and saw me. He made no move to come forward however, but stood stock still until I reached him. Car keys dangled from one hand and he was carrying his laptop under his arm.

'Couldn't you sleep, either?' I said quietly.

He looked me up and down, his face expressionless, his eyes unreadable. I swallowed and ploughed on.

'Josh, there's something I must say to you.' He loomed above me, as cold and remote as a pillar of granite.

'Oh?' He quirked one eyebrow and waited. I swallowed hard. That unblinking stare was making me feel like something that had crawled out from under a stone. 'I shouldn't have thought we had anything to say to each other after last night.'

'That's what I mean.' Then it all came pouring out in a nervous rush. 'That I'm sorry for being so horrible to you. It was unforgivable of me. It was because of the shock, you see, and the mess, and . . . I . . . I just lost control.' I bent my head to avoid the stare, and scuffed the toe of my shoe in the gravel.

'Of course I shouldn't have bawled you out like that. You were, as you said, only looking after our interests.' My voice trailed away. 'And I just wanted to . . . to explain, that's all. And to repeat, I'm sorry I behaved as I did.' An uneasy silence fell.

That was it. Enough grovelling. I'd extended the olive branch, admitted I'd been in the wrong, and now he could take it or leave it. I kept my gaze on the ground as I waited for some response. Above me I could hear keys jingling. Apart from that, silence.

But then came the last thing I'd been expecting. I jumped as I felt a gentle finger beneath my chin, tilting it up until our eyes met. Josh was gazing down at me now with an altogether softer expression.

I felt my heartbeat quicken. For gone was the looming granite spectre, and in its place stood the warm and caring man I knew.

'Oh, Mel.' He sighed. 'I'm sorry too. For shouting at you when you were so shocked and upset.'

I felt my jaw drop. 'You are . . . ? You were . . . ?' I stammered, feeling a sudden lift of my spirits.

Josh nodded. 'And I realise too, how much it must have cost you to come and apologise. I appreciate it.'

I took in a deep breath. It was going to be all right, wasn't it? The dreaded moment had passed and we seemed to be friends again. I heaved a sigh of relief. After all my fears and worries, it was too good to be true.

'I gather neither of us slept well last night.' Josh looked me up and down. I suppose he could see the dark shadows under my eyes that I'd noticed for myself earlier. He too, was looking tired and drawn.

I nodded and smiled. Lost for words to express the muddle of emotions that were going through my head, I changed the subject. The weather was always a safe bet. I indicated the glowing morning. 'But it was almost worth it to see all this.'

Josh seemed as relieved as I was that we'd cleared the air. 'Mmm. It's lovely.' He nodded and paused while his gaze swept over the view.

Then he glanced at his watch. 'I must go, Mel. I thought I'd make an early start as I was awake anyway. I want to get over to the office and do some work before everyone else gets in.'

My head jangling with mixed emotions, I stood for a long moment watching him as he strode away. Then gave myself a shake and returned to face the day in front of me.

7

I was catching up on some neglected bookwork a few days later when Josh came striding into reception and hovered near the desk as if he wanted my attention.

'Er, Mel, I wonder if you can spare a minute? I won't keep you long.'

'Of course.' I glanced at him and noticed with surprise that there were frown lines across his forehead and dark shadows under his eyes, as if he still wasn't sleeping well.

'Is anything the matter?' I eyed him with concern. Closing the register, I pushed it over to one side and leant my elbows on the desk.

'Yeah, I'm afraid so.' He sank into a nearby chair and folded his arms across his chest.

'Something serious, is it?' It had to be, given the anxiety in his expression.

Josh nodded. 'You remember I was telling you about us being pressed for time over making that report about Wheal Hope, and the feasibility of getting it drained and re-opened?'

'Yes, I do. And how you had to get on with the project before they chose the mine in Mexico instead.'

'Right. Well, the thing is, we've searched high and low for the confounded adit or adits, which should be somewhere fairly obvious around here, but are not.' His shoulders heaved and he let out a deep breath in a sigh of frustration.

'Jim and I and the others have quartered the ground around the remains and scanned the cliff-face too. Now we've given it all we've got. The tunnels must have got silted up over the years, I suppose, and are covered with vegetation.'

'And unless you find a drainage point, you can't de-water the mine.' I glanced sympathetically at his despondent face.

'That's it. We can't even bring pumps in to work it from the top, because we don't know how stable the ground is underneath.' He spread his hands in a gesture of defeat. 'It's a vicious circle. I just don't know where we go from here.'

'Oh, Josh, I'm so sorry.' My heart went out to him as our eyes met and held. I had to forcibly restrain myself from getting up and clasping him in my arms, he looked so forlorn.

As forlorn as I was feeling too. For I'd been so looking forward to going out for a carefree evening with him, and subconsciously had been hoping that it would lead to a new closeness between us. I sighed. But he hadn't mentioned another date, so that was not to be.

'And you're sure this is the end? There's no other possibility? Nothing you've overlooked?'

Josh sighed and leaned forward, resting his arms on the desk. 'The only thing we can do is to bring in a more sophisticated ground-penetrating instrument, go over the ground one last time — and hope. If that fails, we'll have really come to the end of the road.' His face fell as he murmured under his breath, 'And the end of all my dreams, too.'

What could I say by way of comfort? There was nothing to say, much as I might wish to.

'It's because of the time factor, you see. We were only given such a small slot in which to work before the developers move in. The minute we move out they can start on their precious new car park and visitor centre.'

'What?' I jerked to attention and my voice rose to a squeak. 'Car park? Visitor centre? What are you talking about, Josh?' I felt my eyebrows climb to my hairline. 'We haven't heard anything about that!'

He looked astonished. 'You haven't?' His eyes widened. 'Oh yes, they were granted planning permission months ago. Weren't you informed at all?'

I shook my head. 'Josh, come with me and tell the others what you've just told me. Please.'

Shock waves were churning through me as my mind raced. Where would it be exactly? How much ground would it cover? How close would it be to us?'

★　★　★

We found Rob and Claire eating a late meal at the kitchen table. They both looked up in surprise as I swept in, followed by Josh, and the door slammed shut behind us.

'Mel! Are you all right?' Claire must have noticed the worry on my face. She straightened, her fork poised over the plate, and frowned. 'What's up, Josh?'

I slipped into an empty chair beside her. 'Josh has just told me some news.' I stabbed a finger towards the window. 'Did you know anything about plans to build a visitor centre over there? And a car park?'

Two blank faces gazed back at me. 'A

visitor centre?' Rob shook his head. 'No, first I've heard of it.'

'So you haven't been told?' Josh said. 'But it's required by law that the dwellings most affected should be notified.'

'How far away will it be?' Claire's fork clattered to the plate as she stared at us wide-eyed in disbelief. 'Will we be able to see it? And why haven't we been informed?' Her questions came thick and fast.

I drummed restless fingers on the tabletop. 'Are you sure, both of you, that if notification came we didn't mislay the letter? It would have been around the start of the season when we we so busy.'

'I certainly don't remember anything coming.' Claire shook her head, pushed back her chair and rose to her feet, leaving the rest of her meal untouched. 'We always put incoming mail on the dresser, don't we?'

I nodded in reply.

She riffled through a bunch of old

letters in the rack there. 'Nothing.' She shook her head and looked back at us. 'Rob, come and help pull the dresser out, in case anything has slipped down behind it.'

Josh stepped forward as well and between them the two men levered the heavy old piece of furniture away from the wall.

'Goodness knows when this was last moved.' Rob stirred a foot in the accumulated dust, getting down on one knee to peer closer. Then he gave a low whistle and paused. 'Well, well . . . '

'Well, what?' Claire and I spoke together. 'Oh, Rob, come on out,' she urged him. 'Have you found something?'

Her husband finally emerged clutching in one hand a brown, official-looking envelope covered in dust and cobwebs.

'Reckon this could be it.' As he brushed it off and waved it in the air, Claire impatiently grabbed the letter out of his hand before he could get up, and ripped it open.

'Oh! It is!' She clapped a hand to her mouth as we read it together, Josh looming over my shoulder.

' . . . any objections to be raised . . . before . . . What's the date today?' Rob reached for the calendar hanging nearby and ran a finger down it.

'Good grief!' He gave a low whistle. 'Friday of last week. They did tell us. But we've missed the chance to object!' He raised grave eyes to us all.

'But there must be something we can do, isn't there?' I looked instinctively to Josh. He would know more about this sort of thing than we did.

But he was slowly shaking his head. 'You could try, I suppose, but I'm afraid you haven't got a leg to stand on, really.'

I recoiled in horror as I had visions of cars revving up at all hours, doors slamming, people shouting, the screams of children. Chaos, noise, all threatening the peace of this beautiful place. After we had worked so hard to make it the haven it was.

'Actually, if you think about it, I imagine it might be quite good for your business,' Josh said kindly. He must have seen the consternation on all our faces. 'A heritage centre or whatever it is. It'll bring people to the area who might not have come this way otherwise.'

I crossed fingers, frantically hoping he was right. 'Well, if the complex is far enough away not to interfere with us, but within walking distance,' I replied grudgingly, 'I suppose you could be right. But I'll believe it when I see it.'

Josh gave me a consoling pat on the arm, and our glances met. His was warm and supportive and he gave my arm a gentle squeeze before letting go.

'Don't worry too much, Mel, until you know for certain.' I returned the gaze until I realised Rob had looked up from the letter and was staring at us.

'There's a plan here as well, look.' He pointed to the diagram that went with it and we all crowded over his shoulder.

'But it comes right up to our boundary fence!' Claire wailed and clutched her husband's arm. 'Look! There's the house, and the track to the cove. The car park will extend to a few yards from our kitchen window. Oh, Rob, that's awful!'

'It's unthinkable.' Stunned by this revelation, I gazed wide-eyed at him. 'So the letter was here all the time, and none of us noticed. That's what's so frustrating.'

I swallowed back threatening tears, then realised the phone had been ringing insistently for several moments before I or anyone else had become aware of it. I hurried back to reception, dealt with the business and leaned forward with my elbows on the desk, my head pounding.

It was only then that I realised Josh had followed me out and had paused beside me. 'I'm really sorry this had to happen for you, Mel. I hope it won't be as bad as you think.'

I nodded. 'Thanks, so do I.'

'And, er, I just wanted to say thanks too, for listening to all my woes just now. I had to talk to someone,' he murmured. 'And you're a good listener.'

A warm feeling spread through me in spite of everything, as he gave me the ghost of a smile.

'I only wish there was something I could do to help,' I replied, holding his gaze. 'But we both seem to have the same problem, in a way.' I shrugged and gave a shaky smile.

'Ah, but there is.' With a sudden lightening of mood, whether real or put on to cheer me up, Josh changed the subject.

'Enough of all our problems for a minute. I'm absolutely famished! I really only came in just now to ask if I could have a sandwich to take back with me to the office. Then when I saw you . . . well, it all took off and I unloaded all my worries. Sorry.' He paused.

'Anyway . . . ' He straightened and

turned on a heel. 'I'll go and find Carol. She'll be in the kitchen, I suppose?'

'Oh!' I jerked back to reality. 'No, no, she won't be. She's already left. I'll come and do it for you.'

'But,' he hesitated, 'I don't want to drag you away from your office work.'

I shook my head. 'I can't concentrate on anything after all that. And it won't take a minute to make you a sandwich.'

It was very quiet in the kitchen. Rob and Claire had gone upstairs and Alex, with Isobel's dubious 'help', had been turning out the garden shed and as yet had not heard the news.

Josh's rangy figure seemed to fill the room and with him looming over me, I heard myself speaking far too quickly as I always did when flustered.

'What would you like?' I asked, flinging open the door of the fridge and stooping to rummage around. 'There's ham, cheese, or both. Pickle, salad? Brown or white bread? An apple or a banana to follow?'

'Whoah there.' Josh held up a hand.

'I can't take all that in at once. Brown bread, please. I've got that. Ham and . . . salad, did you say?'

'Uh, huh.' I nodded over my shoulder.

'That would be good. And . . . um . . . do you have any tomato ketchup?' I caught a shamefaced gleam in his eyes. 'I'm a kid for ketchup, I have it on everything.' He paused. 'And an apple would be fine.'

Josh leaned on the worktop watching as I worked, and his stare was making me all fingers and thumbs.

Then Alex walked in, with Isobel at her heels, both of them streaked with dirt and cobwebs.

'Josh!' Isobel ran towards him. 'Hello, what are you doing?'

'Hello, urchin.' Josh snapped back to his normal self as he smiled. Then picking her up, he swung her off her feet and twirled her around. 'Where've you been, playing in the coal-bin?'

He set her down again. 'No, silly. I've been working. Me and Mummy.' Full of her own importance, Isobel stuck her snub nose in the air.

I was wondering again at Josh's easy way with children, which led to the still unanswered question of his own family, or whether he had one at all.

Alex smiled down at her daughter. 'You should see the stuff we've turned out of that shed!' She went to wash her hands at the sink. 'I shouldn't think it's been touched since Mum moved out of here.'

'No, I don't think it has.' I shook my head.

'Well, thanks for this, Mel.' Josh picked up his food. 'I must go.' He turned to leave.

'You're very welcome,' I said with a smile and raised a hand. 'See you later.'

'Right, young lady, upstairs with you.' Alex gave her daughter a nudge. 'You need a bath and a hair wash.' Isobel made a face, but did as she was told without complaint.

Pausing in the doorway, Alex looked back over her shoulder.

'Talking of Mum, Mel, it's been ages since I last saw her. I thought I might take Izzy over there one day soon.'

'Fine. Yes, good idea. Come to think of it, I haven't either. Seen her for a while, I mean.' I nibbled my lip, thinking. 'I wonder if I could come with you, just for an hour or two.'

'That would be good. And you could do with a break yourself.'

I nodded. 'OK. If Claire can do reception and Carol keep an eye on things . . . As long as we're back to get the evening meal, I will, then. Maybe one day next week?'

Alex nodded and we left it at that for the time being. I would put her in the picture about the development when she came down again.

* * *

I was coming out of the office early one morning, where I had been sorting out old papers and documents and shredding stuff that was no longer needed, when I bumped into Claire in the passage.

She glanced at the bags of rubbish I was carrying and her brows rose. 'Gosh, you've been busy.'

'Yes, I've put this off for far too long. It was getting overwhelming. Now I'm feeling really good, and I know where to find everything again.'

I put the two loaded bin-liners down and paused. 'Claire, I was wondering . . . Alex is taking Isobel to St Ives today to see Mum. Which reminded me when I thought about it, I haven't seen her for ages either — not since the season started, really. We've been so busy.'

'Go as well, then, why don't you?' Claire paused. 'We can manage for a few hours here without the pair of you.'

'That's what I was leading up to.' I smiled at her. 'Well, if you're sure, then I will.' I laid a hand on her arm and squeezed it. 'Thanks Claire, I'll do the same for you one day.'

'How about we do the park and ride and get the train from St Erth?' Alex and I were putting things together to take to St Ives. 'I know we'll have to backtrack first, but it'll be worth it. You'll never park in the town at this time of year and there's that super view as it goes all round the bay.'

'OK. We'll have an early lunch, right? I phoned Mum and made sure she's in.'

An hour later we were boarding the little train.

'Is it as far as London?' Isobel enquired, apprehension in her eyes as she must have recalled the long, boring hours of her last train ride.

Alex and I burst out laughing together. 'No, sweetheart, nothing like that,' Alex reassured her as Isobel wriggled her bottom into the seat and gazed out of the window.

'Look at all those birds down there.' She pointed. 'What are they doing?'

We were passing the estuary of the

river Hayle, where flocks of waders were circling, landing and squabbling over the rich pickings in the silt at low tide.

'They're finding yummy things to eat,' I told her. 'Lovely, slimy things. Like grubs and maggots and worms . . . ' I grinned at her horrified expression.

'Ugh!' She wrinkled up her button nose in disgust. 'Yuck!'

We had soon left the estuary behind and were clattering round the curving arc of pure golden sand, miles of it, fringed by a sea of cornflower blue.

'Ooh, I can see a lighthouse — just over there.' Isobel was kneeling on the seat and pointing back at the way we had come, where Godrevy light perched on a small island at the far end of the bay.

'Here we are.' Alex was gathering their belongings together. 'And don't forget to pick up your bucket and spade, Izzy.'

★ ★ ★

Mum's flat was reached by a steep, cobbled incline leading up from the harbour. Then a flight of steps to the upper storey of a former fisherman's cottage.

'Phew, you must be fitter than I am,' I remarked, out of breath as we at last reached the front door where Mum was standing, waiting for us.

'You get used to it.' She smiled, hugging us in turn. 'Come in, come in. It's so lovely to see you all. I watched you toiling up the hill,' she laughed, her eyes crinkling at the corners.

'I bet you don't miss much from up here.' I peeped through the narrow-paned window at the panorama below, then turned back into the room.

As Mum sat Isobel on her lap and started talking to her, I thought how well and happy she was looking. Her new life obviously suited her.

Tall and still slim, belying her age, her iron grey hair was swept back in a bright bandanna, and she was wearing cropped trousers topped with a paint spattered smock.

We caught up on each other's news over tea and chocolate biscuits, and she was as dismayed as we were to hear about the potential development. But after all that, Isobel was understandably getting restless and we began to make a move.

'Come to the beach with us, Mum?' Alex said, gathering up the bags.

'No thanks, darling. Not today. I've got some work I must finish for the exhibition on Friday.' She gestured towards a pile of canvases just visible through the door of the next room.

'Exhibition?' I chipped in. 'Oh, that's wonderful.'

'Oh,' she shrugged, 'it's only with the local art group I go to. They put one on every year.'

'Lovely. We must come over again before it finishes, and have a look round.'

We took our leave then and headed down towards Porthminster beach. Strolling through the densely packed holiday crowds, with the sun gleaming on the turquoise sea and coloured boats bobbing at their moorings, it felt as if we were on vacation too.

We settled on the beach for a couple of hours while Isobel splashed about in the water and made an elaborate sand-castle with Alex's help. By then she was getting tired and fractious so we packed up and with the promise of an ice cream when we got there, strolled back towards the town.

We walked along by the harbour and found a pleasant café with tables outside, overlooking the bay. Across the road, with their backs to us, people were sitting on the benches and trying to keep the seagulls from swooping on their pasties.

We were watching their antics with amusement, when my attention was caught by a couple with a little boy, below us on the harbour beach.

The woman was stretched out face down, sunbathing, while the man was playing with the child who was about four or five years old.

They had been engrossed in building an enormous sand-castle with a moat around it, and as I watched, the boy grabbed a bucket and ran down to the water to fill it. While he did so, the man rose to his feet, stretched, then turned to his companion with some smiling remark.

Then my stomach gave a sickening lurch as I recognised him. When he half turned and I was certain, my breath caught in my throat and I gasped.

It was Josh. Obviously taking time off for an outing with his girlfriend? Partner? Wife and child? And I'd been feeling sorry for him because he was under such pressure with his work!

Suddenly I was consumed with red-hot, boiling rage. Why hadn't he hadn't had the decency to tell me the truth about his family life and why had he asked me to accompany him to the concert in Truro?

The woman was standing up as well now. I registered long slim legs in white mini-shorts and tumbling blonde hair casually caught up in a clip at the back.

Alex hadn't noticed anything, being occupied with cleaning up Isobel's sticky face, and I didn't point the family out to her.

They were packing up now, ready to leave. I saw Josh and the woman embrace and exchange a kiss, before he went one way and they turned towards the steps below where we were.

I quickened my step, as Alex and Isobel were some way in front of me by now. I'd fallen behind while I'd been staring, and I could hardly linger any longer. Besides, the last thing I wanted was for Josh to turn round and see me.

So as I trudged behind the other two up the steep hill to the station, I was in a world of my own, still fuming.

Thinking back, hadn't Josh said his home was in Saltash? And that it was too far to commute while he was working down here? So the woman and child must be down on a day trip, or here for the weekend. Josh would hardly have been staying with us if she was here for any length of time, would he?

I was trying hard to come to terms with reality as I dragged my feet up the slope.

Men, I railed silently, they were all the same, never to be trusted. Yes, Josh had a partner. Of course he did, I'd always assumed so, hadn't I? But until I'd actually seen her, I thought he might have been different from the rest, and there had been a small flicker of hope. Now there was nothing left.

8

Since that day, I had been trying to empty my mind of all things personal and get on with the hundred and one tasks waiting to be done at the hostel. We were coming up to the busiest time of the season.

Our rooms were comfortably full, with more reservations on the books to come. With a couple of birdwatchers, four people on a walking holiday together, and two families with young children, the time was taken up with stocking up on supplies and cooking numerous meals each evening.

The arrangements were that our guests served themselves breakfast each morning in the residents' kitchen. If they wanted a packed lunch they must order it the night before, which most of them did, and very few came back during the day. This meant that we could catch up on jobs like laundry and cleaning while they were away.

Of all our guests, Josh was the only one who came and went at odd hours as, of course, he was the only person not on holiday. We had become so used to having him around the place the others treated him as almost part of the family. But I could never think of him in that way. Far from it. He had a more special place in my heart, no matter how much I tried to fight it.

Anyway, I was not surprised to see his car draw up one weekday morning, as Claire and I were pegging out washing on the long line down the side of the garden.

'Hello you two,' Josh called, slamming the car door and heading our way. 'Nice weather for it.' He grinned and nodded towards the line of laundry crackling and snapping in the breeze.

'Hi, Josh.' We smiled and waved. 'I don't suppose you've heard anything about the development, have you?' I asked him over my shoulder. 'We've been looking in the local paper, but there's been no mention of it.'

Josh shook his head. 'No, I'm afraid not.' He came and stood beside us, rocking back on his heels, hands stuffed in the pockets of his jeans.

'Actually, I . . . um . . . I wanted to ask you both something. Well, all of you really, Rob too.' I glanced up at him and wondered what was coming.

'Oh, yes?' Claire picked up the empty basket and we both waited for him to carry on.

'It's just that I was wondering if you'd all like to come down to St Ives for a barbecue on the beach at the weekend.' He paused and cleared his throat.

'My family are down for a break, and I thought we could have a bit of a party. Two of my work mates are coming along as well.' He paused. 'Only if you'd like to, that is. And if you can spare the time from the hostel. I know how busy you are.'

I felt my heart churn at the words

'my family', and recalled with hurt the smart woman and laughing little boy I'd already seen him with at the beach.

Oh no! There was no way I wanted to go on this trip. In fact it was the last thing I'd choose to do. I'd give anything to wriggle out of it. Could I plead pressure of work? That I was needed here? But I knew my sisters. If they decided to go, they wouldn't let me stay behind. It would make them feel too guilty.

'Oh? That sounds a great idea.' Claire was smiling up at him. 'We'd love to, wouldn't we, Mel?'

'Well, er, um . . . we'll have to get cover for what has to be done here . . . ' I stammered. She raised her eyebrows and gave me an odd look.

Josh smiled. 'You don't need to give me an answer right away. I knew you'd want time to think about it and make arrangements. So just let me know when you've decided.'

★ ★ ★

Alex was highly enthusiastic about the trip of course, as I'd known she would be. She'd become used to London life, having lived away for so long, and found the pace of things down here a bit quiet for any length of time.

'A beach party? Brilliant!' Her eyes sparkled. 'We'll be able to go, won't we?'

Claire too was keen. 'I could drop in and say a quick hello to Mum while we're over there, couldn't I?' she said, animated. 'That would be good — I haven't seen her for ages.'

'Well, I'm quite happy to stay here and hold the fort,' I said brightly, crossing my fingers behind my back. 'I was over there recently. And I saw Mum then as well. Besides, I never was much of a one for parties.'

They both stared at me as if I'd suddenly grown two heads. 'Of course you're coming, Mel.' Alex looked me up and down, wide-eyed. 'We wouldn't dream of going without you, would we,

Claire?' She turned to her sister for support.

'No, absolutely not.' Claire shook her head. 'Alex is quite right.' She fixed me with a determined look and wagged a finger.

'Now listen to me, Mel Treloar. Rob will be at home as it's the weekend. He and Carol can manage perfectly well without us. The residents can have a cold meat salad for once. It's summertime, after all. Isn't that right, Alex?'

'Perfectly. There is no reason whatever, Mel, why you shouldn't go off and enjoy yourself as well.'

Oh, yes there is! I wailed inwardly. *If you only knew* . . . But I pasted a smile on my face and shrugged. 'Oh, well, then, if you're sure . . . '

I knew when I was beaten. I heaved a sigh. All I could do now was pray for rain.

* * *

It didn't happen, of course. The morning dawned cloudless and sunny, with a gentle breeze from the south-west. A perfect day for the beach. After the long spell of almost unbroken rain we'd had earlier in the season, it seemed we were having a heatwave now to make up for it.

We were ready soon after lunch, all of us in brightly coloured summer tops, and a selection of shorts or cropped trousers.

Rob came to the door to see us off. 'You lot are looking like a bed of flowers all blowing in the wind!' He smiled broadly.

We laughed out loud. Rob, so solid and matter-of-fact, was not normally given to sentiment.

We loaded up the boot of the car with the amazing amount of baggage one needs for a day on the beach, and all piled in.

Claire was driving, with me beside her and Alex and Isobel in the back. We rarely went out all together, I usually drove myself, but today I had a chance to enjoy the view, which was fantastic.

As the switchback road climbed and twisted, I could see a patchwork of tiny fields spread out below, reaching as far as the sea in the distance. Edged with dry-stone walls, they dated from medieval times. Behind us, the huge crags looming on the other side of the road were infinitely older. The standing stones, quoits and rounds among them were so lost in the mists of time, no-one could even tell for certain why they had been built.

Seen from the hill above the town as we approached, St Ives was lying in a pool of sunlight, a gem encircled by the sapphire sea. And as we parked the car and unpacked our belongings, I felt my spirits begin to lift in spite of myself. It was impossible to stay downhearted in such a place, on such a day.

Weekend crowds were thronging the streets, weaving in and out of the shops, viewing the exhibitions in the artists' studios, or just relaxing on the several beaches. We had arranged to meet Josh on Porthminster sands.

I spotted him right away, my eyes instantly drawn by this inner magnetic force over which I had no control. Sometimes I even found myself wishing he would walk out of my life for good and leave me in peace, for the constant push-pull of our present situation was leaving me emotionally drained.

However, I was equally aware that some time not far away he would be leaving for good. The job would soon be over and I would probably never see him again. Then I would have plenty of time to regret my present thoughts. I heaved a sigh and trailed behind the others down the steps to the sand.

Josh and his friends were kicking a soft ball about, the little boy doing his best to join in. Not far away, a female figure beneath a large straw hat lay sunbathing. As Josh caught sight of us and called a greeting, she slowly sat up and removed her sunglasses as we approached.

Josh picked up the ball and tucked it under his arm as he came to meet us.

'Hi there! Good to see you all.' He smiled and beckoned. 'It's a great day for it. Come on over and meet everybody.'

'These are my work mates, Jim and Mike.' I smiled and held out a hand as Josh introduced us. Jim was about Josh's age, Mike more mature, bearded and greying.

'We're just off for a swim,' Jim replied. 'We'll catch up with you later.' They waved and strolled off towards the water.

The little boy was now clinging to Josh's free hand. 'And this is young Jake, my other mate.' He grinned, swinging the child off his feet so that he laughed with delight.

Seeing Isobel watching them, wide-eyed, he tossed the big ball towards her. 'Catch it, Izzy!' he called. 'Oh, well done!' The child's face lit up with glee as she managed to clasp it in both hands before it hit the ground, then grinned at Josh in triumph.

'And this is Sue over here.' We'd reached the patch of rocks where all their belongings were strewn around, and dumped our own stuff beside it. I recognised the blonde hair and white shorts from the first time I'd seen this woman, and recalled the fury I'd been in. Now I had to spend a whole day in her company.

'These ladies are Claire, Alex, Mel and Isobel.' Josh sprawled himself on the sand, as we said our hellos and I pasted a polite smile on my face.

'Lovely to meet you.' Sue smiled warmly. 'And to have some feminine company too. I've been feeling really outnumbered by all these men.'

'Well now we've really turned the tables on them.' Claire smiled back, as she and Alex spread out the rugs we'd brought, and we all sat around soaking up the sun.

Porthminster was a long arc of gloriously golden sand, sheltered from the wind by the bank of buildings above it, with all the amenities needed for a perfect family holiday.

I lay back and closed my eyes against the sun. The others could be sociable, I was opting out of the chit-chat and would join in only when strictly necessary.

'Uncle Josh! Uncle Josh!' Distantly I heard a child's voice floating towards us across the beach. But it was only when Jake came running up, closely followed by Isobel, and they kicked sand all over my feet, that I raised my head.

It took a few minutes to sink in. Sun-soaked and dozy, I shook my head to clear it, and wondered if I'd heard properly.

'Will you help Izzy and me make a sand-castle? The bestest castle ever. With a moat, and water, and . . .'

He flopped down onto the sand. 'Mummy, I'm hungry. Can Iz and me have a biscuit? Please.'

'Oh, Jakey, don't you ever stop eating?' Sue sighed and reached for a bag. 'Have a banana for now. And give

Isobel one.' She turned to Alex with a smile. 'Is that OK with you? We'll get ice creams later, Jake, if you're very good.'

'My sister is very particular about what children should and shouldn't eat.' With a start, I found that Josh was lounging beside me, his back against a comfortable rock, and gently teasing Sue. 'Sweet things are strictly rationed, and have to be earned by good behaviour.'

Sue, retaliating, playfully threw a child's flip-flop at him. It caught Josh on the side of the head and she burst out laughing. 'Behave yourself, little brother, or no ice cream for you!'

Stunned, as I watched and listened to this banter in disbelief, the shock still hadn't fully registered. His sister?

My jaw dropped. And I'd thought . . . but it was understandable . . . he hadn't actually said, had he? And I'd assumed . . . on the beach that day, looking like any other family . . .

I bit down hard on my lip. And I'd

been so angry that day. All for nothing. I'd made a fool of myself again. But only to myself. Thank goodness I hadn't been seen. And that I'd never told anyone. Especially Josh! I cringed at the very thought of what might have been.

'Sue's your sister?' I murmured, almost to myself, but loud enough for Josh to jerk round and look at me in surprise.

'Of course she is. Who did you think she was?'

'Oh, it was just a misunderstanding on my part.' I shook my head as warmth flooded my face, and tried to shrug the whole thing off. 'Only you never actually said so, you see.'

Josh's eyes bored into mine and the corners of his mouth twitched. He knew. Or guessed. Oh, no! But to do him credit he didn't actually laugh out loud at my mistake.

'You thought she was my wife? Or girlfriend, didn't you? And that Jake was mine?' The half-smile vanished as he put a hand over my own and gently squeezed it. 'Oh, Mel, I'm so sorry. I just didn't realise . . . '

'It's all right. It doesn't matter. Forget it.' My cheeks flaming even more, I shook my head again and withdrew my hand. Claire on my other side was speaking to me now and the embarrassing moment was over.

★　★　★

Forget it, I'd told Josh, hadn't I? But all through the rest of the lovely day and the evening barbecue that followed, I certainly couldn't forget it.

So, was he single after all? Surely it would have been the natural follow-on to my mistake to tell me if he wasn't. So as far as I knew, he was. And my mood began to lift.

By the time the sun had sunk into the western sky in a glory of peach and pink, my spirits had soared, rising with the moon now climbing to its zenith in the velvet sky above us.

We had all fallen silent, seduced by the beauty of the evening, the children half-asleep, curled up at our feet.

Josh was lounging a few inches away from me, and in the twilight his eyes as they met mine, were veiled and mysterious. I wondered what he was thinking.

When Mike produced a guitar and softly strummed it, it was the perfect climax and I wished the enchanted night would never, ever end.

★   ★   ★

Next morning however, the cold light of reason dawned. So Josh was unattached, or seemed to be. But this, I argued to myself, didn't mean a thing as far as he and I were concerned.

Josh had never given me the slightest inkling that he felt anything for me other than friendship. Except that one time he had asked me out, which had come to nothing. Obviously he had changed his mind, as the invitation had not been repeated, much to my disappointment.

Last night's euphoria disappeared with the morning mist. Nothing had changed. I was no further forward and was never likely to be.

★   ★   ★

Sam came to pick me up as arranged for our trip, and after we'd exchanged initial greetings we were just moving off in her car when Josh emerged from the house and strode off towards the mine.

I noticed Sam give him an appraising look, then she did a double-take, narrowing her eyes for a longer stare.

'He's quite a dish, isn't he?' she murmured. I smiled at her natural reaction to any attractive man. Or one of her 'pebbles on the beach' as she called them.

'Oh, that's Josh Stephens. He's working round here and staying at our hostel.'

'Josh Stephens, did you say?' She

braked and whirled round, astonishment written all over her face.

'Ah, yes.' I gazed back at her. 'What do you mean? Do you know him?'

'Oh, Mel,' she gave me a pitying look. 'You must have heard of him. No?'

I shook my head.

'But everyone's heard of Joshua Stephens. He used to be a famous sprinter. He won medals and trophies all over the UK. His face was always in the papers a few years ago.'

I must have still been looking bemused. 'I believe he did mention he used to go running,' I replied feebly, 'but I didn't know . . . I'm not a sporty person like you are, Sam. I don't follow sports news at all.'

'Good grief, even living out in the sticks like you are, I would have thought . . . ' she bit her lip, 'but I suppose Josh would have been at his peak when you were still in London and going through that thing with David.' She grinned. 'So I'll forgive your ignorance.'

I smiled and saw this as a chance to do a little fishing. 'You don't, er, know anything about his personal life, I suppose, do you, Sam?'

She glanced at me over the top of her sunglasses and chuckled. 'Why, do you fancy him? I wouldn't blame you if you did, Mel. He's gorgeous.'

'Oh, just wondering,' I shrugged. 'He's staying with us indefinitely, until his work's finished here. But he never talks about himself.'

'I can't really remember. He dropped out of the sports scene quite early on. I believe there was some story about him and a girl once.' She frowned in concentration. 'It was splashed all over the papers at the time, like it is with celebrities. Like I said, I can't remember what it was. It was years ago.'

She nibbled her lip in thought. 'I believe it was after the — um — incident that his name faded away from the sports scene, and I never heard anything more of him.'

'And you've no idea what the

incident was?' I kept my voice casual, but inside I was mentally urging her to think.

Sam shook her head. 'No. Too long ago. A lot of water under the bridge since then.' She shrugged, then tutted in annoyance. 'Oh, bother. Look at that!'

A tractor had pulled out of a field gateway just ahead and was taking up most of the narrow road. Sam was forced to slow down behind it and its trailer, laden with freshly lifted, earthy potatoes. She sighed as she tapped a polished pearl fingernail on the steering wheel, and I couldn't help but smile, although the moment had been lost.

'It's no good getting uptight,' I told her. 'You're in Cornwall now. The pace of life is much slower down here than in the city, you know.'

'Of course. I do know. And I'm not really fazed. For a minute I forgot I'm on holiday, that's all.'

'Well, you might as well pull in for a minute to let him get ahead. You'll never be able to overtake. The road's too full of twists and turns. With a bit of luck he'll turn into a farm soon.'

'OK.' She stopped the car in a field gateway and switched off the ignition. 'It was interesting to see Josh Stephens though. What sort of work is he doing?'

'He's a geophysicist apparently. Working for a mining company that's surveying the old workings around here.'

'Oh. Serious stuff, then.' She wrinkled up her nose. 'Though it's a far cry from the sporting world that he came from.'

I nodded. 'I think that tractor's turning off now. Up there, look.' I pointed a finger. 'Let's go.'

We pulled out on to the road again and drove along in silence for a while, until I felt Sam give me a sideways glance.

'Mel, are you all right?' she asked. 'You've gone very quiet.'

I'd found myself going over the unpleasant scene with David again, not

169

that I wanted to, but my mind wouldn't let it rest.

'Oh, it's just that something happened the other week.' I shrugged and managed a smile. 'I'll tell you all about it over a long lunch.'

'Oh, right. I thought we'd stop at that little pub in Zennor. I passed it on the way over. I suppose you know where I mean?'

I nodded, my spirits beginning to rise as we drove further along the twisting, switchback road between moor and sea, and I noticed for the first time what a glorious day it was.

A little later, we were relaxing in the sunshine, cold drinks in front of us, at a table outside the pub.

9

'You know, you haven't told me what we're actually going to see.' I looked up from my crab salad and smiled. Sam's eyes crinkled at the corners and raising a hand to her forehead, she pushed back her curly fringe and held it there for a second.

'Oh, no, I completely forgot! I booked at such short notice that all I could get was Gilbert and Sullivan. I hope that's OK by you, Mel.'

'Oh, that's fine.' I nodded. 'Which one?'

'It's HMS Pinafore.' Sam paused, her soup-spoon halfway to her mouth.

'Oh, great. I shall enjoy that. I can do with some really lighthearted fun.' I smiled at her across the table.

'So what were you going to tell me?' Sam looked up expectantly at her friend.

'Oh, yes.' I toyed with a bread roll, absently crumbling it as I spoke. 'Well, David suddenly turned up out of the blue.'

'David?' Sam spluttered over her soup. 'But I thought you finished with him ages ago.'

'So did I.' I picked up my fork and speared a mouthful. 'But he wanted us to have another go at making it work.'

'Oh, Mel, you're not going through all that again, are you?' Sam gazed at me in concern.

'No, don't worry.' I shook my head and smiled at her. 'I sent him packing.'

'So I should hope. After the way he treated you.'

'It wasn't easy, Sam. There was still a bit of the old attraction there, you know?' I let the fork slip from my hand, reliving the scene. 'Until he let slip that he was in Penzance anyway, and I realised he hadn't come especially to look me up. And that did it. I saw red and bawled him out.'

'Good for you. Well done.' Sam gave

a nod of approval. Then she put down her spoon and glanced at her watch. 'Hey, we ought to be going. You have finished, haven't you?' I nodded, pushed back my chair and followed her out to the car.

We thoroughly enjoyed the performance, but who wouldn't, in such a glorious setting in near-perfect weather? Below us the white sands of Porthcurno beach gleamed in the sunshine, bathed by a calm turquoise sea. But for the temperature, we could have been in the Mediterranean.

The theatre was so cleverly constructed it gave the impression of being part of the natural cliffs and as we perched on the circle of grassy seating, the scent of wild gorse and thyme wafted on the breeze around us. For a couple of hours I was completely transported out of myself and my problems, into the fantasy world of Captain Corcoran and the 'Queen's Navee!'

173

* * *

A few days later, I met Josh in the passageway as he entered the side door when I was on my way to reception.

'Oh, there you are, Mel.' He smiled broadly. 'I was just coming to find you. I'd like to take that box file back from your office if it's convenient.'

'Of course.' I turned and retraced my steps. 'I'd forgotten all about it.'

'I hadn't forgotten, but there wasn't any urgency for it after all and I just haven't got round to picking it up.'

As I turned towards the shelf, Josh laid a hand on my arm. 'Hang on a minute, Mel. After what happened last time, I think I'd better get it for myself!'

'Oh, yes. Good idea!' I laughed and stood back as he reached down the file. Then casually as he was about to go, he unexpectedly remarked, 'How did you enjoy your trip to the Minack the other day?'

I replied with enthusiasm. 'Oh, very much. It was wonderful. The play was hilarious and so lighthearted it really cheered me up.' I looked up and smiled. 'You know what a perfect place it is down there, how romantic it can be, don't you? And of course, the weather was lovely too, really warm and sunny.'

'Has your city friend gone back home now?' He gave me a long stare.

'Oh, yes.' I nodded. 'We had a good long chat and a catch-up, but Sam only had the weekend, before going back for work on the Monday. We're hoping to have a few more days in September though, when we're less busy here. I might even go up to London to stay. Have a bit of holiday, I thought.'

I tidied a few papers I'd disturbed as I passed and put them into the desk drawer. 'Oh, yes, Sam and I have a lot in common. We go back a long way, to when we were both working in a London hospital.'

I glanced up with a smile and noticed, puzzled, how Josh's expression had changed, just as if a shutter had suddenly come down. I wondered what he was thinking. About his problems at work, no doubt.

Trying to snap him out of it I said brightly, 'And you? What was your concert like? Did you enjoy it?'

'I didn't go,' he grunted. I raised my eyebrows in surprise. And though I waited for him to explain, he didn't elaborate.

I was just about to ask why not, but it wasn't really my business. And as we left the room I wondered what was making him so moody. I searched my memory in case I'd said the wrong thing, but I couldn't think of anything that would account for his sudden coolness.

I shrugged as we parted in silence and thought no more about it.

★   ★   ★

A few days later, we'd been sitting in the dining room, all of us having had lunch together, which was quite unusual. Rob's building firm had just finished one job and not yet started on another, and he'd come back early to join us. We'd just started moving to and fro clearing the table, taking the dirty dishes back to the kitchen between us, when Rob rose to his feet and pushed back his chair.

'While I've got an hour to spare I thought I'd put a coat of paint on the . . . ' But he broke off in mid-sentence as we suddenly heard the strangest noise.

It was a loud crack like gunfire, coming from outside, and followed by an ominous rumble like the onset of a massive thunderstorm.

'Good grief, what on earth is that?' Alex and I stared at each other wide-eyed, as the reverberations rolled around between sea and sky.

'Outside — come on.' I grabbed her hand and we ran towards the front door.

'Mummy, Mummy, I'm frightened!' Isobel came charging out of the kitchen, followed by Carol, wiping her hands in her apron as she went, then Claire. Alex swept the child up in her arms and we all dashed outside.

A huge plume of dust was rising over the sea, birds were flying up screaming at the disturbance, and the roaring had intensified. We ran as far as the picket fence at the end of our property, then stopped abruptly.

We were in time to see a huge chunk of the cliff below the house slowly detach itself from the rest. For a second, the piece of land stayed upright and intact, like a slice of cake, before crumbling away almost in slow motion. Then it slid towards the churning water with a roar like a wild animal, breaking up into hundreds of tons of debris as it went crashing into the sea.

Previously there had been about a hundred and fifty yards of wild and rocky moorland between the cliff-edge and the hostel. Now, beyond a mere fifty or so, there was nothing.

The land-slip had taken a huge bite out of the cliff face and spat it into the foaming water. Small rocks were still tumbling down over the scree, and at its foot the sea was churning up a paste of soil, sand and debris.

'Oh, my god!' Claire clapped a hand to her mouth, her eyes popping. 'Look at that!' She clutched my arm as we all stared in awe at the scene of devastation.

I swallowed hard. 'It must have been all that rain we had back at Easter . . . '

Alex nodded. 'That probably loosened the soil . . . Now with the heat-wave . . . '

'It often happens,' Carol said quietly. 'I actually noticed a great crack in the ground only yesterday. I was on my way up here, but I didn't think anything of it at the time. But to be so near the house . . . oh, my!'

She put into words what we all must have been thinking. How would this affect us?

I was still staring into space, shell-shocked. At the newly-formed edge of the land, torn and mutilated roots of heather and other bits of vegetation were waving pathetically in the breeze. But gradually the rumbling died away and the dust settled. Birds returned to their business, bees buzzed in the remaining stands of heather, and a couple of butterflies oblivious to all the drama, alighted on a bush beside us. Nature had returned to normal.

But we had not. Far from it. For the effects of this were going to be enormous. And the more it sank in, the more trouble I could see looming. We turned and walked slowly back to the house in silence.

As we were going inside, Rob detached himself from the group and walked round to the back of the house, while we went in through the front.

'I'm going down to the cellar to have a look around,' he said over his shoulder. 'I suppose it's too soon to look for cracks, but you never know . . . ' He went off, muttering to himself. I caught the word 'subsidence' and shivered.

The rest of us filed into the kitchen

and stood around in a huddle, too shocked to think straight.

Subsidence. The word echoed round and round in my head. It was inconceivable. This great granite house had stood for over a hundred years. Its cob walls were two feet thick, its enormous beams supported a roof of solid Cornish slate. After over a hundred years standing four-square to all the worst weather the elements could throw at it, how ironic it would be if nature was at last getting its own back.

When Rob returned a few minutes later, all our eyes turned to him. I noticed how slowly he came in. How he closed the door carefully behind him. How hunched his shoulders were. This was so out of character for the big man who normally strode whistling about the house, slamming doors regardless, that I could tell how worried he was.

He thrust a hand through his hair and I could see that his normally ruddy face had paled. He slowly shook his head. 'Couldn't see anything. But,' he drew a deep breath and looked round at us all, 'I could hear the sea booming when I was down there. We never could before, could we?' He paused to let this sink in.

'It sounds as if it's directly below the house.' Rob gazed around at all our stunned faces. 'Of course it isn't, else we wouldn't be here now.' He summoned up a weak smile. 'We'd be floating.' He spread his hands wide as nobody laughed. 'But it'll need to be investigated, of course.'

I swallowed hard and blinked. 'You mean . . . you seriously think . . . we're being undermined?' My voice rose to a squeak and I felt my eyebrows arch to my hairline.

'I don't know, Mel. I glanced at the walls and I can't see any cracks. But like I said, it's too early yet to be able to tell.' He heaved a sigh. 'I'll go back and give it a thorough going-over when it's had time to settle.' Solemnly our eyes met and held.

'We'll have to get a surveyor in though, to do a proper check, won't we?' Claire frowned and bit her lip.

Rob nodded. 'As soon as possible.'

At that moment we heard a shout at the open back door and Josh came striding down the passage.

'You've seen it, of course.' His face was strained and his eyes serious.

We all nodded dumbly. I licked dry lips. 'We're just trying to think what it means for us, and what to do for the best.'

'And I'm worrying about bookings.' Claire nervously fiddled with a lock of her hair, then tucked it behind her ear. 'We're fully committed, practically all season.'

'That's something I've just been thinking about too. You being responsible for other people's safety.' Josh looked solemnly around at us all.

'I've walked all over the remaining ground, examining it between the house and the cliff edge.' He slowly shook his head. 'And I don't want to sound alarmist, but I wouldn't guarantee its safety. There's a hollowness about one particular place that I'm not too happy about at all.'

My heart turned over. I swallowed hard and glanced at Rob.

He was nodding in agreement. 'I went down to the cellar, Josh, and I can hear the sea from there.'

'That would be the place, then.' The two men stared at each other in mutual understanding.

Josh glanced around at us all. 'And, given that you are as I said, responsible for the people staying here, I'm wondering whether you ought to evacuate them. Until we know how safe the house is.'

'Evacuate?' My voice rose to a squeak. 'B . . . but, where to?' Shock had blanked out coherent thought and for a moment I couldn't think straight. Then my business brain took over and started whirling.

Meanwhile Claire was murmuring away almost to herself, thinking aloud.

'We would have to ring around all the guesthouses we can find. In Penzance, St Ives, any holiday cottages that have vacancies . . . ' She was biting her lip as she gripped the back of a chair like a lifeline and gazing unseeingly out of the window.

'But at this time of year it's bound to be tricky.' Alex was clasping Isobel to her for comfort. 'They'll be as busy as you are. Besides which, think of the huge cost involved.'

Rob sank into a chair that creaked in protest at his weight, and Josh took a seat beside him.

'Now let's think this through.' Rob drummed his fingers on the table top. 'Mel, how many guests do we have staying here at the moment?'

'Er . . . ' I conjured up the register in my mind, that was now functioning more normally, and managed a mental picture of the bookings. 'I'll have to check of course, but I know the two families are leaving tomorrow,' I murmured, thinking hard. 'That's convenient, it only leaves, um, six, I think.' I counted them on my fingers. 'Those two bird-watchers and the four walkers. Oh, and you, Josh, of course. Seven, then.'

'Don't worry about me,' he flapped a hand and summoned up a smile. 'I'll go and sleep in the office if I have to.'

Claire was clasping her arms around herself as if she was falling apart. 'Six,' she repeated, frowning.

'Well, that's not too bad,' Alex put in. 'Surely you can find alternative places for six, even if they have to split up.'

I nodded, nibbling a thumbnail. 'Oh, I hope they won't be too upset and make trouble. And that they won't spread rumours too, that we're unreliable. It could mean the end of the business . . . ' I heard my voice quaver.

'And that's not all.' I turned towards Rob as tears threatened. 'We shall have to cancel, or postpone, future bookings too. For the next — what — how long . . . ?'

Rob raised an eyebrow and glanced over at Josh, who slowly shook his head.

Rob spread his great hands and shrugged. 'We just don't know, Mel.' He fell silent, a frown creasing his forehead.

'You'll have to get them all together and explain what's happened,' Alex put in. 'They'll have seen the fall, anyway, and realise the position you're in.'

'And if you do have to evacuate,' Carol broke in, 'what about yourselves? You're going to have to move out too, don't forget.' She stood with folded arms, looking at us with concern.

'Oh, goodness, I hadn't thought of that! I suppose we will.' I turned to Rob and raised anxious eyes to his.

'You're welcome to come and stay with me,' Carol went on. 'It'll be a squeeze but we can manage somehow, with temporary beds. There's even the loft . . . ' Her brow furrowed, already making imaginary arrangements.

'Oh Carol, that's sweet of you.' Claire squeezed her hand. 'I'd like to say we wouldn't dream of bothering you, but it's difficult to know anything at the moment.' Her voice trembled.

Then Rob rose to his feet, put one arm around my shoulders, the other around Claire's and gave us each a gentle squeeze.

'We'll get through this, girls. You'll see.' I could tell he was trying to lighten the atmosphere and comfort us with false heartiness. 'I'm a builder,' he smiled, 'trust me. That right, Josh?' He winked at the other man. Josh, preoccupied, nodded curtly in reply.

Trust him? This was hard to do. As I leaned into his comforting arm, my mind was reeling with wild visions of all our hopes and dreams crumbling to dust, just like the land we'd been standing on such a short time ago.

'What happens next?' Claire drew away, chewing a fingernail. 'Shouldn't we call the police? Before anyone falls over the slip? It took a chunk of the footpath with it, don't forget.'

'Yes.' Rob nodded firmly. 'Good thinking. You're absolutely right. I'll get on the phone this minute.' He left the room, heading for the reception area.

'And I must get back.' Josh rose. 'I left the others waiting for me. I'll see you all this evening.'

He left the way he'd come and the rest of us fell temporarily silent, locked in our own thoughts.

Alex was the first to speak. 'And how are you going to find a surveyor? Where do you start? Does anybody know?'

'Yellow pages?' Claire suggested. 'Or the Health and Safety people may have a suggestion?'

'They'll come last, won't they? To inspect it after we've had it checked?' I suggested, moving to put the kettle on. Tea — the automatic comfort in times of trouble. 'Maybe the internet. Google even?'

The shock we'd had must be wearing off. For as we were returning to normal, everyone seemed to be talking at once.

'Better still,' Rob chipped in, returning to the room. 'Haven't we got a professional surveyor staying under our very roof?'

I felt my jaw drop. 'Josh, you mean? But you can't ask him!' All sorts of thoughts were crowding my brain at the very suggestion.

'Why not?' Rob raised an eyebrow in surprise.

'B . . . because . . . ' And as my hands moved automatically, filling mugs with tea and handing them round, I really couldn't think of any logical reply.

'I'd hate to say that he owes us.' Rob shrugged. 'For rescuing him that night I mean, and normally I'd never mention it, but well . . . ' He drummed his knuckles on the arm of his chair.

'But you can't say that to him!' I blurted, horrified and as my hand shook, I slopped tea all over the wooden table-top. I hastily reached for a cloth. 'Rob, you can't possibly!'

'Of course not.' Rob shook his head. 'Not in so many words, I mean. But in a roundabout way, if I have to.' He drew his tea towards him. 'Although I'm sure he'll understand, and probably offer to do it anyway, without me having to ask.'

'But Josh is under tremendous pressure with his own work. He told me so.' I slid into a chair, took a sip of my own tea and clasped my hands around the mug for comfort, resting my elbows on the table. 'Do you really think it's fair to ask him? Because he's bound to feel obliged to, if you put it like that.'

'Well, he can always say no, can't he?' Rob swallowed his tea in a couple of huge swigs, put the mug down and headed for the door. 'I'll see if I can catch him before he goes.'

10

How different a man's attitude is compared with that of a woman, I thought, glancing at Rob's broad, retreating figure. Finer feelings don't come into it with them.

'Anyway,' he called back, 'right now I'm going out there to cordon off that area with rope and put up some temporary warning signs, until the authorities take over. They'll have to put up official notices and re-route the cliff path.'

'Who actually does own that land?' Alex queried, as Rob strode purposefully away.

'It'll be the National Trust, I expect,' Carol replied. 'Most of the coastline round here belongs to them.'

'If anybody fell over, would they die?' Startled as the small voice piped up, I glanced at Isobel's little white face and frightened eyes. I'd forgotten what a huge impression this must have made on her, especially seeing all our worried faces.

'Nobody's going to fall over, sweetheart,' I reassured her. 'Uncle Rob has gone to make sure of that.'

'If you listen,' Claire added, 'you can hear him hammering in the fence posts now. Can you?' The child cocked her head on one side as loud thumps could be heard coming from beyond the end of the garden, then she solemnly nodded.

'And Iz, listen to me now. You must never, ever, go outside the garden to play unless somebody is with you.' Alex set her daughter on her feet and raised a finger as she looked steadily into her face. 'Stay inside the fence. Do you hear me? And do you understand?'

Isobel stared up at her and nodded again. Poor little kid, I thought, feeling sorry for her. She and the dog were used to romping everywhere with no restrictions, except that she stayed within sight of the house.

Carol, who had been quietly listening and watching, now tactfully changed the subject.

'Well,' she announced, putting on a cheerful face, 'I thought I might do some baking today.' She reached for her apron on its peg behind the door. 'I wonder if anyone would like to help me?'

The simple ruse worked instantly. 'Me! Me! I will!' Isobel sprang to life and was halfway across the room before Carol had finished speaking.

* * *

Rob must have met Josh somewhere outside, as later I saw them both come back together and lean over the picnic bench, poring over a map Josh had spread out in front of them.

I was on my way out with some scraps to put in Jess's feeding bowl, and lingered beside them on the way back.

As I raised a hand to shield my eyes

from the sun, I realised what a glorious summer day it was. Beyond our fence, a sheet of tiny blue squill flowers poured across the turf like water, and in the distance, butter yellow kidney vetch was cascading down the cliff beyond the slip. Some late primroses and a few hardy bluebells winked among the green shoots of new bracken, nestled in sheltered spots beneath the boulders. High above I could hear the tumbling song of a couple of larks, lost in the blue infinity of sky. Then I looked at the devastation of the cliff fall and my heart sank.

'Oh, Mel,' Rob glanced at me as I tipped the food into the dog's bowl. Behind Josh's bent head he gave me an enormous wink, 'Josh here has offered to use his instruments to help us check the area around the house.'

'Oh, that's wonderful!' I feigned surprise. 'Really kind. Especially as I know how busy you are, Josh.' I tried to imply that we weren't taking him for granted.

'No problem,' he replied. 'I'll find the time somehow.' He turned and our glances met. 'After what you both did for Chris and me when we were in such trouble with the boat, it's the least I can do in return.'

Oh, how formal and polite we are, I thought. It's like some elaborate dance where we're all trying to avoid treading on each other's toes. I'd dearly like to know what Rob actually said to Josh before I came out. And what Josh's real feelings are, behind the bland façade.

'Of course,' Josh was saying, 'you'll have to get someone else in to examine the inside of the house. I'm a geophysicist, and my tools are only calibrated for land research.'

He folded up the map and stood up. 'I'll have to go into Penzance and get some stuff from the office before I can start. I left my laser range finder there last night.'

'Your what?' I asked, bemused.

'Oh, sorry. Technical term.' A flicker of a smile crossed Josh's face. 'We use ground penetrating radar equipment in my job. This is portable, computerised equipment. More accurate and much less cumbersome to carry around than the old instruments.'

He stood up and started walking towards the car. 'I'll get some of the team to help me, starting first thing tomorrow morning.' He glanced at his watch. 'I really must go. Until this evening, then.'

★ ★ ★

I went back inside to find Isobel standing in the kitchen doorway. 'Oh, there you are, Aunty Mel, I've been looking for you everywhere.'

'Yes, here I am sweetie.' I bent to her level. 'What did you want me for?'

'Come in here.' She stood back and grabbed my hand, pulling me inside.

'Look what I made, all by my own self!' Proudly she waved a hand towards the tray of sickly-looking cupcakes on the table. Carol in the background gave me a wink and a thumbs-up sign. 'Go on, Aunty Mel, have one.'

'They look lovely, sweetheart.' I glanced at the inches thick icing, decorated with as many varied sweets as she'd been able to cram on top, and accepted the least calorie-laden one I could find. 'Mmm.' I took a sticky bite. 'Yummy. Well done, you. Thank you very much.'

The child took her own cake and went off outside with it.

'Well done, Carol, too,' I said with a smile. 'That was an inspired idea. And they're really very nice underneath!'

She chuckled as I reached for a knife and scraped off all the gooey topping.

★　★　★

I found it hard to concentrate on anything for the rest of the day, and I'm sure the others felt the same. The worry of what Josh and his men might or might not find tomorrow was at the forefront of all our minds, even pushing the hovering threat of the new development to one side.

And I kept imagining the worst, however much I told myself to wait until I heard the results. If we had to close down the business, if the house was classed as so unsafe we had to move out permanently, what would I do?

Claire and Rob would be all right. He had his job; they could easily find somewhere else to live. Alex was going back to her life in London with her husband and child soon, anyway. Carol had her own home.

But me? I would lose my home and my job. I would have to go back to nursing in order to earn a living. The thought was far from appealing. It would be the most tremendous wrench. Just as I'd made a life for myself here after the last upheaval. But of course it might all fold even if the house did remain stable. If this pending development encroached so much that the business had to close, there would be nothing left here for me after all. Between a rock and a hard place, then.

And anyway, where would I go? Never back to London, certainly. But the need for qualified nurses was universal; I could go anywhere I chose. I had visions of facing a bleak future. Staying single, for I had lost all faith in men, becoming more and more lonely as I grew gradually older, with nothing in my life except my work . . .

Oh, for goodness sake, pull yourself together and get your chin up off the floor! I snapped out of my misery as I caught sight of my doleful face in the mirror of my room, and laughed instead. Nothing had happened yet, and fingers crossed, it might not even be as bad as we feared. But . . . whistling in the dark, they called it, didn't they?

11

Josh was as good as his word and turned up early next morning. Hearing a noise, I glanced out of the kitchen window to see the truck draw up, then the three men all wearing yellow dayglo jackets began unloading various items of equipment. Josh tossed them each a hard hat and they dispersed around the cliff top and started work.

'What are you looking at, Mel?' Claire came and stood beside me, lifting back the kitchen curtain for a better view. 'Oh, they've started. What's Jim doing, though? Looks like he's coming back.'

'I suppose he forgot something.' I was turning away, but she clutched my arm and pointed. 'No, Mel, look, he's got a huge coil of rope in his arms. And now he's tying it round the bumper of the truck.'

'Oh, yes.' I peered through the window again and frowned. 'But why is he walking away with the rope again? And uncoiling it as he goes?'

'Simple.' We both jumped as Alex appeared out of nowhere and joined us. 'If you look at Josh over there,' she pointed to the far edge where the landslip was, 'he's putting on a harness. I'd say he's going to abseil down the cliff face and take readings from below.'

'Abseil!' I gasped. 'But isn't that dangerous? Going hand over hand down that sheer drop?'

'Oh, Mel, for goodness sake!' Alex turned to me with scorn. 'You don't think this is the first time Josh has ever done that, do you? In his sort of job? Oh, come on.'

She was right, of course. It was only this heightened sensitivity I felt around Josh that was making me so jittery.

'And it's certainly not dangerous if the person takes the right precautions, and has the correct equipment, which

I'm sure he has. And I speak from experience.'

'Yes, I suppose you do, Alex. I was forgetting you must have done it yourself.'

'Frequently,' she smiled, 'and survived to tell the tale, as you can see.' We all turned back to the scene beyond the kitchen window.

'I don't know what Mike's doing, either.' Claire frowned. 'What's that thing he's pushing along?'

I followed her pointing finger.

'I've no idea. It just looks like a lawn-mower with a screen on the handle.' She laughed.

'Ah, now Josh did mention something about a ground penetrating radar,' I added as an afterthought. 'Maybe that's the way it works.'

Claire withdrew from the window. 'Well I really must get on, there's masses to do and Carol's a bit late this morning.'

She glanced at the wall clock. 'Oh, here she is.' She smiled as Carol came bustling in.

'I stopped to watch the goings-on,' she said, reaching for her apron. 'This is the survey, I take it?'

'Yes. They'll test the stability of the ground. But we've still got to get someone in to give the house a thorough check.'

I frowned and passed a hand over my forehead, where a headache was threatening. The lack of sleep, combined with the worry over the house and the strain of my preoccupation with Josh, were all taking their toll.

'Of course.' She nodded. 'Now, how many residents are here this morning? Has anyone left?'

'Nobody,' I replied. 'None of them wanted to go, even after yesterday's events. They're all serving themselves breakfast.'

'Oh, that's good.' Carol's expression relaxed. 'I'll push the cleaner round in there when they've all gone out.'

'And I must check the supplies too, and make a shopping list. Now we're so busy we get through such a huge amount of stuff really quickly.' Claire went off to the big utility room where we kept our stock.

'I'll come and help you.' Alex followed her out of the room. 'Izzy seems quite happy at the moment. She's in the sitting-room, talking to her toys and watching the men outside.'

'Well, I've got accounts to do' I turned towards the office as we all drifted off to do our separate chores.

The idea was not appealing, as half my mind was wondering what was going on outside, and with my underlying headache I found it hard to keep my attention on the registers. I worked for half the day then packed it in and took on something less demanding.

★   ★   ★

I was finishing some ironing in the kitchen when I glanced out and saw the men coming back, one of them coiling up the rope as he came.

As he untied it and tossed it into the

truck, Josh removed his helmet, threw it after the rope, then did a thumbs up to the others as they drove off.

As he came striding towards the house, his laptop under one arm, I hurriedly switched off the iron and went to meet him.

'Josh is back!' I called as I passed the sitting-room, where Claire and Alex were playing a board game with Isobel. Carol had finished for the day and gone home, Rob was not yet back from work.

'Hi Josh, how did it go?' He looked tired out, but gave me a smile as he passed a hand through his unruly hair.

'I'll come in and explain,' he said, as we joined the others. Josh gave a sigh, sank into an armchair and stretched out his legs in front of him.

'Well, I can't tell you much about the actual ground survey at the moment, until we study the findings,' he admitted.

I felt a stab of disappointment, but of course, they would have to look at all the readings before they were sure.

'But anyway, when I abseiled down the cliff to the beach this morning, I did discover something.'

Wide-eyed, we all craned forward to listen.

'You know that big cave you call Kit's Cupboard? That's been silted up for so long?'

I nodded.

'Well, it's amazing.' Josh spread his hands for emphasis. 'The slip has taken away all the debris that was blocking the entrance and swept it clean away. It's completely empty — you can walk right inside now, and it's huge, really huge.'

'Really?' Claire and I both spoke at once and sat up straighter, then laughed.

Josh glanced down at Isobel standing at his side, solemnly listening. 'I didn't see any sign of old Kit's treasure though, munchkin.' He grinned. 'Maybe next time.'

'Ooh! Can I come with you next time?' Her whole face lit up at the idea. 'Please Josh?'

'Perhaps. But first I'll have to find out whether it's too dangerous.' He playfully ruffled her hair and turned back to us.

'Anyway, the thing is,' the serious expression returned to his face, 'I'm pretty sure that's why you can hear the sea from your basement. The cave goes back so far it could run directly underneath it.'

'Underneath the house?' My voice rose to a squeak. 'Oh, no!' As I felt my jaw drop, I could see my horror mirrored in the faces of the others. I gulped, my lively imagination already painting mental pictures of the hostel and everything in it tumbling headlong into the sea.

At that moment, Rob put his head around the door, saw us, then advanced into the room. Before he closed it, Isobel, obviously bored with all the adult talk, picked up her doll and slipped out.

'I wondered where you all were. It's so quiet in here.' Rob glanced around at our shocked faces and sat down. 'What's going on?'

As Josh repeated his story and explained the situation, Rob's ruddy face paled and he gave a low whistle.

'B-but,' he stammered, 'how much danger do you think the house is actually in? Can you tell?'

Josh leaned forward, forearms on his knees. 'I walked inside the cave as far as I could before it narrowed, and had a thorough look around. The roof of it seems pretty sound as far as I could see. At a guess I'd say it's not in imminent danger of collapse. I also climbed up on the highest ledge I could find and tested with the portable kit I had on me.'

'Mmm, I see.' Rob nodded, frowning. 'So basically, we just don't know.'

Josh shook his head slowly. 'Not until I can get to the office tomorrow and put together all the surface readings we took as well. Then we can get a broader picture of what's going on and decide what action to take. I'm afraid they've closed today, the staff had to go to a funeral.'

Josh shrugged. 'I'm sorry I can't tell you anything more definite for now.'

We all fell silent. I could almost feel the tension crackling in the air as we each locked into our own thoughts.

Then I jumped, somewhat startled, as Josh's voice broke into my reverie.

'As well as that, Jim discovered there's a biggish crack in the soil further over. I took a look at it and I'm pretty sure there's another chunk of cliff ready to fall soon. Nothing like as big as the first, but it looks as if a good push would send it over. It is quite near the cliff path though. It ought to have a warning sign put on it.'

'Another one?' Claire sat up straighter and her eyebrows shot up. 'Is it likely to affect us at all?'

'No, no.' Josh reassured her. 'Don't worry. It's way further off from the house.'

'Phew!' She sat back in her chair, as relieved as I was to hear this. 'Thank goodness for that. We've got enough to think about already.'

Nobody had a lot to say after that, as we went our separate ways. We could only cross our fingers and hope, as we waited for tomorrow's results.

★ ★ ★

'Mel, I don't suppose you've seen Isobel anywhere?' Shortly afterwards Alex put a worried face round the door of the office, where I'd gone to file the rest of the correspondence I'd abandoned earlier.

I looked up and shook my head. 'No, not since she left the sitting-room. Why, can't you find her?'

Alex bit her lip. 'No. I've been looking everywhere. And calling.' She shrugged. 'But she seems to have just vanished.'

'Don't worry. I expect she's hiding away somewhere, thinking it's a great game to fool you. She'll turn up when she's hungry, I'm sure.'

I finished my work and as I left the room a few minutes later, I heard Rob's voice calling from outside.

'No, Alex, she's nowhere out here.'

'And neither is Jess.' That was Josh's voice. So he must be looking for the child as well. 'Wherever Isobel has gone, I bet they're together.'

This seemed to be getting more serious than I'd thought. I went out to join them.

'You still haven't found Izzy, then?' This was worrying now as more and more time passed, although I wouldn't say as much to Alex.

But she was worried enough already. As she turned to me I could see how pale she was, and close to tears. She shook her head and I squeezed her shoulder for comfort.

'I told her the other day,' Alex's voice wobbled, 'you heard me, didn't you, Mel? Told her not to leave the garden unless someone was with her. But she must have done. Why would she now, after all this time?'

I shook my head, bemused. Then suddenly something clicked in my mind. I gasped as I clutched at Alex's arm.

'Listen! I've just thought of something.' Our eyes met and held. 'When was the last time you saw her?'

Alex's white face was a blank. She slowly shook her head. 'Um . . . In the sitting-room — when Josh was talking to us.' She bit her lip. 'Then she slipped out. I haven't seen her since.'

'Exactly. And Josh spoke to Izzy then as well.' I shook the arm I was holding. 'Do you remember? He made a joke about Kit's treasure?'

Alex gulped. 'Mel — you don't think . . . she's gone out . . . over there . . . to look for herself? Oh, my god!' She covered her mouth with both hands, then raced down to the end of the garden with us at her heels, and peered over the fence.

'Rob! Where are your binoculars? Quickly!' I called as he ran to the garage and grabbed them from the back of the car. He tossed them to me, and shading my eyes against the sun I scanned the horizon, anxiously looking for any movement.

And there in the distance I could make out a small figure in a red top marching across the cliff. My heart turned over.

'Izzy!' I gasped as all the air left my body. The child was making her way purposefully towards the edge of the cliff, with Jess capering about behind her. As I watched, she stopped and peered over the edge.

'There!' My voice came out as a croak as I turned to the others. 'There she is!'

They came to a halt and followed my pointing finger. Josh grabbed the binoculars from me and put them to his own eyes.

'Oh, no!' His sudden shout was right in my ear and I flinched. 'She's heading straight for that new crevasse!'

Alex let out a piercing scream and clutched at me as her knees buckled.

Josh was already vaulting over the fence. Then gathering speed, he ran.

As I watched Josh covering the ground like a hare with the hounds on its tail, I could hear Sam's voice again, echoing through my mind.

Oh, Mel, everyone's heard of Josh Stephens . . . he used to be a famous sprinter . . . And Josh's own more modest remark, *I used to do a bit of running myself.*

Now I could well believe it.

Alex and I set off right behind him. Both of us were pretty fit, but Josh was almost out of sight behind the scrubby gorse bushes in the distance before we were halfway.

Rob had stayed to get out the car, a four-wheel all-terrain vehicle that would drive over anything, and Claire was with him. Alex had refused to wait for the lift and I was so worried she might collapse on the way, I felt obliged to go at her pace. However fit she might have been, at the moment I could see that her legs were like rubber.

We stumbled on, panting for breath. Stones, roots of heather and patches of prickly gorse all combined to slow us down. Then in the distance I saw Josh take a tumble as he tripped over something and went down full length on the ground.

'Oh, no!' I gasped. Was he seriously hurt? What if he'd broken something? My heart thumping even harder, I kept going. But he must only have been winded, as he was up again in a moment, arms akimbo, head thrown back, seemingly drawing in deep breaths of air. Then he was off again.

And I had almost caught up with him. When I'd seen Josh fall, I'd put on an extra spurt and had left Alex then to catch up in her own time.

Now, from a few yards away, I could see Josh slow down as he came within reach of Isobel and begin to creep slowly up behind her.

Horrified, I understood.

The child was standing on the far side of a huge crack in the ground. Any sudden noise or fright and she could fall either into the crevasse, or plunge straight over the edge of the cliff.

My heart in my mouth, I could hardly bear to look. But neither could I bear not to.

Isobel had stopped to pick wild flowers. There was a stand of ox-eye daisies and tall foxgloves growing on the patch of turf at her feet. Obviously she had given up any hope of seeing the treasure cave and had been distracted by the flowers instead.

As I watched, unaware I was biting my thumbnail down to the quick, she tugged at a tough stem of foxglove, lost her balance and sat down hard on her bottom, inches from the cliff edge and totally oblivious to the danger.

I heard a whimper behind me and a hand slip into mine. Alex had arrived, taken in the scene and was standing speechless, shaking with terror at my side.

Josh was now standing at the thinnest end of the crevasse, one foot on the solid land as he gingerly tested the ground on the other side and eased his weight on to it. He was over and gradually inching towards the child, who was still unaware of his presence. Isobel had stayed in the sitting position and was playing with the flowers in her hand.

Josh must have quietly called to her, for she turned round and looked over her shoulder. Then suddenly, he grabbed her round the waist with both hands. As the child screamed, with a gigantic heave, Josh tossed her towards us over the crack, clearing it by a matter of inches.

'Izzy!' Alex fell on her daughter and dragged her further back to safety, tears streaming down her face. Then pandemonium broke out. Isobel was shrieking with fright, the dog barking and jumping about from one to the other of us, not understanding the excitement, and at that moment Rob and Claire zoomed up in the Land Rover, drawing to a halt with a squeal of brakes.

With all this racket going on, it was a few seconds before I registered another underlying noise. A roaring, and a grating, followed by a wild shout from Josh.

While our attention had been focused on Isobel, the crevasse had opened, the loose material had broken away and the whole lot was now tumbling towards the sea, taking him with it.

I was the first to be aware of what was happening. I screamed then and raced to the edge, threw myself flat on my stomach and peered over. For a moment I couldn't see anything for the clouds of dust rising, but as it settled I could see him.

Josh was lying immobile on a ridge of rock where he had come to rest on a ledge about halfway down the cliff.

Lumps of vegetation that had fallen with him were littered around the scree, and stunted roots and branches of gorse were sticking out at odd angles, like pleading arms praying to the sky.

12

It had all happened in a matter of seconds. I glanced over my shoulder. The others were still fussing over Isobel.

I saw Claire just getting into the vehicle and I ran towards her yelling. 'Claire, throw me the first aid kit . . . Josh . . . ' I pointed. 'I'm going down there.'

'Mel, no, you can't!' Rob had seen the situation and was at my elbow, holding me back.

I squirmed from his grasp and shook him off, as the first aid bag came hurtling through the air towards me. I caught it and slung it around me as I ran towards the fall.

'Josh is hurt,' I shouted, 'maybe seriously. I can tend to him. You call for help.'

I looked over the edge again, my

heart in my mouth. The stuff had stopped falling now, but it looked terribly loose. One false move would have me hurtling to my death. I swallowed hard and frantically planned my route, before Rob or the others could stop me. They hadn't as yet seen the fall and had no idea how dangerous it was.

Just below where I stood I could see a ridge of solid bedrock. I followed it with my eye. It seemed to go round in a bend that would avoid the worst of the loose stuff and bring me to the far side of the ledge where Josh was lying.

Now I could hear pounding feet behind me, and shouts. The others were coming. I stepped over and tested the rock with one foot. It didn't move. I clutched at a firmly rooted heather bush and placed my other foot beside it. I was over, and facing the dizzying drop. Far below, the sea boiled and churned, drawing me towards it.

No! Don't look down! said a warning voice in my head, and I turned my face towards the cliff. I looked for the next handhold, thanking providence for the trainers I'd put on that morning instead of the flip-flops I usually wore around the house.

I found a tough root of gorse nearby. Ignoring the thorns that lacerated my palms, I clung to it like a lifeline. The rock still seemed to be solid. I crept downward for a few more feet.

Now it was getting broken up into ridges like small steps. But it was still holding, and there were crevices I could cling to.

The bag on my back was getting heavier with each step, and sweat was pouring down my face and into my eyes. But there was no way I could let go to wipe it off. I paused to take in a deep breath and crept on.

My progress was agonisingly slow, but I dared not try to hurry. Snatching a sideways glance, I could see I was now approaching the end of the shelf where Josh lay. But there was a pile of loose fallen stuff to cross before I could reach him.

Licking dry lips, I left the relative safety of the rock and released one hand to grab one of the broken roots and branches sticking out of the cliff face. Praying it would hold my weight, I stepped out onto the scree.

Shaking so much I nearly let go, I gingerly reached for another branch. In one moment of blind panic, I felt the fallen stuff shift beneath my feet, and gave a sickening lurch.

I clung on like a limpet, hanging above the sheer drop, tears streaming down my face, waiting for what must come. But my feet steadied, and held. There must be bedrock under the broken shale.

As I shuddered and gasped for breath, my terror eased just the slightest bit. I was making progress, in fact I'd almost reached the far end of the ledge.

At last I could actually touch the turf. I clutched at a huge cushion of tough thrift and with one arm around it, I managed to pull myself up until I was kneeling on the grass beside Josh.

Now waves of dizziness and nausea swept through me. I couldn't lift my head as sea and sky whirled around me in a blur. I stayed motionless until it steadied, then raised an arm to wipe the sweat and dust from my face.

Absently I noticed that Isobel's flowers still lay scattered where they had fallen, incredibly undisturbed by the slip. This chunk of ground where the drama had first begun had amazingly stayed intact and upright as it broke away and dropped. If it hadn't . . . I trembled to think where Josh might be now.

By now, I'd recovered enough to crawl over to where Josh lay immobile. Still, he was so still. My heart lurched as I imagined the worst. I slipped the first aid kit off my back and placed a hand on his forehead. It was cold and clammy with sweat.

Concussion? I bit my lip. If so, he shouldn't really be allowed to sleep.

Check his heartbeat. Where was it?

Frantically I put my ear to his chest. Nothing. I took hold of his shoulder and shook it. 'Josh, wake up. Josh!' But it was useless, he was out cold.

Then my professional training kicked in. This was no longer Josh lying on a precarious ledge hanging out over nothing. This was a patient. Right. Keep calm. And don't look down.

I cupped his face in my hands, gently lifting his eyelids to check the pupils. If he was concussed they would be dilated unevenly. But his eyes seemed normal enough and I gave a sigh of relief.

Now however, I could feel a lump on the side of his head, which had until now been hidden by his hair. So that was why he'd passed out. Did he have any more injuries? I bit my lip as I unzipped his jacket and slipped my hands inside to feel up and down his ribcage. I massaged his heart and put my face to his chest to listen for a heartbeat.

It was there, but thready. I kept up the massage. But even then, with Josh perhaps critically ill, even then my body was subconsciously responding to the feel of his warm skin beneath my fingers.

As I moved, my lips accidentally brushed against his cold ones, and I had to resist a strong temptation to linger there. I tore my mouth away, lifted my head, and saw Josh's eyes, wide open and fully awake, fixed on my face.

How long had he been awake, watching me? I felt my cheeks flame as I sat back on my heels, staring speechlessly at him. There was a blankness about his gaze, but oh, the relief at seeing him conscious at last!

'Josh!' I gripped his hand. 'Are you all right? Oh, I was so worried!' I reached for the first aid kit. But Josh had turned his head and was struggling to speak.

'Mel!' he stammered. 'Wh — what on earth . . . ?' He struggled to sit up, didn't make it, and sank back with a grunt.

'You've had a knock on the head,

Josh, from the rockfall. But don't worry, you're going to be all right now.'

My voice cracked on a sob as tears threatened. Relief, joy, and the release of tension were all combining to make me feel weepy. But I swallowed hard and blinked them away. We were a long way from safety yet.

Josh was still struggling to sit up, but the professional in me placed a firm hand on his shoulder and pressed him back onto the grass. 'No, lie flat. You must rest.' Far better for him not to know how precariously we were perched, and what danger we were both in.

Josh sighed as he sank back, and raised a hand to his temple. 'Oh, good grief, yes! Isobel. It's all coming back now. Is she all right?'

'Perfectly. You saved her life, Josh.' *And nearly lost your own*, I thought to myself.

'But where . . . where are we now?' His forehead puckered in a frown. 'I remember falling . . . the ground gave way . . .'

'We're going to be all right.' I reached for a pad and the water bottle. 'Now I'm going to clean that bump on your head, and dab some antiseptic on those scratches on your face. It might sting a bit.'

I rinsed my own hands with a drop of the precious water, and took a few sips to ease my parched throat. Never had water tasted so good. I could have drunk a bucketful. But I mustn't have any more. It was only a small bottle.

Josh flinched as I wiped away a little blood, then placed a cold pad on his temple and bandaged it.

'Are you feeling warm enough, Josh? You mustn't get cold.' I fussed about with his jacket, which I'd undone to get to his chest. I zipped it up again as far as it would go, and turned up the collar.

Then Josh turned his head, shot out a hand and grasped my wrist, pinning me still so that I couldn't stop him from raising his head and glancing around. 'Right, now where exactly are we?' He caught sight of the yawning abyss below us and his jaw dropped open.

'Oh, my god!' His eyes met mine. 'Mel! What happened? Tell me. How did you get here? I don't understand . . . ' He frowned, trying to concentrate, then winced with pain. 'Ouch! My head's hurting like hell.' He released my hand and fingered the bandage.

'I'll tell you later, Josh. It's a long story. You need to rest. The others have sent for help. Someone will be here soon.'

He frowned again, but the effort to think was too much. The small amount of colour that had returned to his face was fading again, and he was obviously still in shock.

'Listen!' I raised a hand as I heard the roar of an engine above us. 'There's a helicopter hovering up there.' I shaded my eyes and squinted, as it came a little lower. 'I think it's coming for us! Hang on in there, Josh. They'll soon have us out of here.'

★   ★   ★

All through the rescue procedure I was functioning automatically. Now that I could off-load the responsibility on to someone else, my brain seemed to have shut down completely. I'd done all I could do, and now I was suddenly overcome with exhaustion. I was also aware of my aching legs and my own cuts and bruises.

I felt as if I was never going to have the strength to move again. The fatigue I knew, was caused as much from the release of strain as from the result of my climb. Adrenaline had kept me going long enough to do what had to be done. Now that had drained away, I was ready to collapse.

They sent down a man on a rope. I registered him putting a harness on Josh and taking him up and away. Then they came back for me. I must have said I was all right, for after a brief check, he lifted me off the cliff and lowered me back to where the others were waiting. Then I passed out.

13

I remembered very little of the rest of the day, until I came round in my bed next morning. Then the events of the previous day came flooding back as I stretched my stiff body and staggered out to the bathroom.

I met Alex coming out of it, still in her dressing gown and slippers like me, as I was going in.

'Ah, at last!' She smiled as our eyes met. 'Good morning, Rip Van Winkle.'

I gaped at her. 'What do you mean, 'at last'?' I glanced up at the clock. 'It's only just gone nine.' I frowned at her. 'Considering what I went through yesterday, I don't think — '

'Mel,' she said, her eyes sparkling with mirth, 'that wasn't yesterday. It was the day before yesterday!'

'What?' I stared at her in disbelief.

'We all took turns to look in to see if

you were all right. But you obviously needed it, so we left you in peace.'

I felt my eyes widen. 'No wonder I'm starving,' I said, as my stomach gave a rumble.

'How are you feeling now?' Alex looked me up and down with concern in her eyes.

'Fine, I think. My legs are dreadfully stiff and my hands are sore, but that's all. What about Izzy?'

'She's OK, apart from scratches and the odd bruise. She had a bad fright, but children soon bounce back.'

'And Josh . . . how's he?' I blurted, thinking of the pale, suffering face I'd last seen on the cliffs. 'And where is he? Still in hospital?'

'Yes. I phoned them yesterday. He's OK in himself, they say, but he's being kept in for another night for observation.'

'You haven't seen him, then?'

'No.' She absently rubbed at her damp hair with the towel she was carrying. 'I asked if I could, of course, but he wasn't being allowed visitors until today.'

'Shall we go in this afternoon, both of us?' I stepped past Alex towards the bathroom door and pushed it open.

'I can't today.' Alex shook her tousled head. 'I made an appointment for Izzy to have her hair cut this afternoon, and mine as well.' She ran a hand through the unruly mop, leaving it standing on end. 'I can't really break it, as the hairdresser put herself out to fit us in at short notice. But you can go.'

She paused for a moment. 'Perhaps you could give us a lift on the way to the hospital? I was going to get the bus, but it's so slow. Would that be okay? Do you mind?'

'Of course I will. No problem at all.' Privately I was pleased to be able to go on my own.

Alex chewed her bottom lip thoughtfully. 'Mike was talking about going in to see Josh later this evening. I might go over with him, after Izzy is in bed, as I want to thank him personally. If he hadn't . . . '

'I know.' I squeezed her arm as I headed for the shower.

★ ★ ★

Josh was sitting up in bed when I arrived, gazing into space, an unread newspaper beside him. There were visitors beside every bed but his, and the ward was alive with chatter. The way his face lit up when he saw me coming made my heart race for a moment, but I told myself he'd been looking so bored, he was probably glad to see anybody. Even me.

The smile was still on his face as I reached his bedside and stood beside him.

'Mel!' Josh sat up straighter and ran one hand through his hair. 'Oh, it's so good to see you. Sit down.' He pointed to the chair beside him.

'Hello, Josh.' I was feeling awkward at how best to greet him. In most situations I would have bent over to give a friend a hug, and a kiss on the cheek. But we weren't really close enough for that, were we? Although, after all we'd been through, surely more than acquaintances. So I gave a mental shrug and gently squeezed his hand before sitting down.

'Well, how are you after all the ordeal?' I looked him over with concern, but his face had colour and animation. Apart from the dressing on his head, which was twice as big as my original one, he seemed his old self, and in good spirits. His lips, which had been so blue last time I saw him, were now pink and healthy looking again.

'Fine, apart from this.' He raised a hand to his head.

'Oh, very piratical.' I smiled, and pulled the chair closer. The ward was so full of chatter I could hardly hear him.

Josh's eyes met mine, then all at once he leaned over and grasped my hand in both of his.

'I'm alive, Mel. And it's all thanks to

you. If you hadn't acted so swiftly, and so bravely, I might not be here now to tell the tale.' His face darkened. 'Being out of it like I was, I could so easily have rolled off that ledge, and . . . ' He spread his hands.

I felt my face flame. He squeezed my hand hard, then released it. 'They told me in A&E what happened. I don't know how to begin to thank you.' His gaze still riveted on my face, the moment lengthened.

We were so close I could smell the scent of his warm skin, and the freshness of his newly-washed hair that was almost touching my face. It was warm in the ward and Josh had bared his torso and pushed down the bedcovers as far as his waist. A swathe of little dark hairs curled down his chest and disappeared beneath the covers. His proximity was having such an effect on my body that I forcibly made myself sit back and take a deep breath.

I swallowed hard. 'You don't have to. I'm only so thankful I knew what to do.'

I smiled and broke the eye contact. If I hadn't, there was a strong chance I would have thrown myself onto the bed with him.

Hastily changing the mood I said lightly, 'Do you remember much about what happened after you threw Isobel over to us?'

Josh took a deep breath, reliving the horror. 'The chunk that was loose suddenly gave way under my weight, then dropped, taking me with it. Miraculously it stayed more or less in one piece. Then all the loose stuff went hurtling past, and over me, some of it bouncing off my back and head. It seemed to go on for ages, but it couldn't really have been more than a few seconds.' He spread his hands wide and took in a breath. 'It was terribly hard not to let go and be swept away with it.'

'What a lucky escape you had,' I whispered, inadequately.

Josh nodded. 'As soon as most of it had fallen, I found the ledge was big enough and seemed stable enough, to take my weight. I stayed on my knees, holding on like a limpet. I've never been so thankful to be hugging a cold, damp rock in my life.' A weak smile crossed his face.

'Then I felt dizzy and passed out. I must have lost my grip, because when I came to I was lying on my back and you were leaning over me.' Josh paused and gave me a long look. I flushed. That was when he must have felt my lips on his.

'There's still a lot I don't know about.' He frowned. 'I can only vaguely remember you being there on the ledge with me. They say you climbed down the cliff, but you couldn't have done that, could you? Not over all that fallen stuff.' He shook his head irritably. 'You must have come with the rescue team in some way. Oh, hell, I'm all mixed up in my mind.'

Then hesitantly, I told him the whole story. As I was speaking, his face registered amazement, disbelief and admiration in turn. He hung on my every word and heard me out in silence.

And as I finished at last, he let out a deep breath and reached for my hand again, covering it with both his own. 'Oh, Mel, I can hardly believe what you did.' As his eyes looked deep into mine I felt colour flood to my face again, and bent my head to break the contact. It was more than I could bear to be so close to him, but also so far away.

'You're a heroine. You deserve a medal.'

'So do you,' I replied, raising my head. 'You saved Isobel's life, remember.'

'She's OK, is she?' Josh's voice was beginning to fade. I could see by now there were faint smoke-blue shadows underneath his eyes and he was losing the colour in his cheeks. It was time for me to leave and let him rest.

'Perfectly. Alex will be in to see you later to thank you herself.' I stood up and placed a couple of paperback books on the bed. I'd almost forgotten I'd brought them.

He leaned over and gently squeezed my arm. 'Thank you so much for coming, Mel. As well as everything else.'

Our faces were very close, I could feel his breath against my cheek, and for a second, as his face softened in a smile, I wondered whether . . . but no. Josh withdrew, leaving my arm feeling strangely cold, and sank on to the pillows again.

'I hope to be back soon. They mentioned letting me out of this place tomorrow or the next day, all being well. So,' he raised a hand, 'it's goodbye for now, Mel.'

I turned and waved as I reached the door. And the memory of Josh's smile stayed with me all the way down the stairs.

★ ★ ★

When Josh was discharged a couple of days later, he returned to the hostel itching to get back to work.

240

'Of course I must!' he growled that evening when I joined him in the residents' lounge, and told him not to rush it.

Although so much was hanging on the report we were waiting for, I didn't want him to plunge in and overdo it before he was completely over his ordeal.

'Don't fuss, Mel! Look at all the time I've lost!' He spread his hands, palms up. 'I must get to the office and get those readings done for you.'

'Well, if you're sure you feel up to it. But it's only been a few days — and we haven't subsided yet!' I kept it light, while mentally agreeing with him. For we didn't know how much time we did have left.

'As for your own work, Mike told me how well your team has been getting on with it while you were in hospital. Didn't you, Mike?' I looked over my shoulder as the big man arrived just at that moment.

'Didn't I what?' he boomed and sank into a comfy chair beside Josh.

I smiled at him as I was moving away to leave them to their chat. 'I was telling Josh that the work hasn't stopped just because he's been laid up.'

'No way! And I came to tell you we've found something really interesting, mate.' Mike leaned forward, elbows on his knees, his bearded face alight with excitement. 'You stay too Mel.'

I drew up a chair as Mike ran a hand over his bearded chin and took in a breath.

'When we saw how much stuff that latest landslip had shifted, Jim and I went down and had a look around.'

He paused and drew in a breath. 'And I could see an opening in the cliff face that I think could be an adit.' He looked Josh in the eye.

Josh suddenly straightened. 'What? You did? An adit?' His face lit up with a huge grin.

'Hold on,' Mike cautioned, lifting up his hand, 'I only said I think it could be.'

'That's good enough for me.' Josh

gazed at him, eyes sparkling. 'And if . . . if it is . . . it would be the answer to all our prayers.' He went on muttering, almost to himself. 'It could only be connected with Wheal Hope — it would be the one I knew ought to be there somewhere, but couldn't trace. I told you, Mel, didn't I?' Biting his thumb, he turned to me in excitement.

I nodded, recalling the time he had confided in me how worried he was. 'You're a good listener, Mel . . .', he'd said. I hadn't forgotten that moment of closeness between us, brief though it had been.

'Or it could be just any old hole in the cliff.' Mike reasoned. 'Until we get the climbing gear and go up there, I'm keeping an open mind.'

'Oh, wow!' Josh's eyes widened. 'I must get over there. Take me in the truck, Mike. Now. This I must see.' He shifted in his chair and made to get up, then winced.

'No, not now, Josh, please,' I pleaded with him and laid a hand on his shoulder, pressing him back in his seat. 'Leave it till tomorrow. Look, it's getting dark.' I pointed towards the window in exasperation. 'It's too silly for words. You tell him, Mike.' I looked at him to back me up.

'Yes, Mel's right.' The big man nodded. 'Tomorrow it is. That hole's been there for at least two hundred years. It's not going to go anywhere overnight.'

Josh's shoulders slumped as he heaved a sigh and sat back in the chair. 'OK, I suppose you're right.' His face fell. 'I must get into the office first thing, but it shouldn't take long to line up those results and get a print-out. Then right after I get back, we'll go. OK?'

'OK. I'll be here, I promise.' As Mike did a thumbs up, Josh relaxed and smiled at last.

★ ★ ★

We still had to find a surveyor to check the interior of the house, of course.

Everything had been put on hold during the emergency. But next morning, Rob got on the phone to a firm in Truro before he left for work, and arranged an appointment.

After Josh had left for the office, I drifted around, not able to concentrate on anything until he came back with the precious report. I was just making coffee and talking trivia with Carol in the kitchen, when I saw the car pull up.

Claire and Alex were bringing in laundry from the line and raised a hand as they saw him too. Hurriedly bundling it into the basket, they followed Josh inside and we all met in the kitchen.

I was trying to read the situation by his expression, but he was purely businesslike and preoccupied as he opened his briefcase and brought out several sheets of paper. We all gathered round as he laid them out on the big table.

'The technicalities might not mean much to you, actually,' Josh began, smoothing out the papers. They were covered in maps, diagrams and cabalistic figures, which, as he said, were not easy for us to understand.

'But anyway, what it boils down to is this. From the information these charts give us, we can tell for certain that the ground is stable.' He looked up with a smile as we all gave a collective sigh of relief.

'Oh, that's wonderful!' I breathed, as we all started talking at once.

When the babble had died down, Josh went on. 'All that loose stuff that's fallen is just what it appeared to be — loose. But beneath it there's solid bedrock. Solid as a . . . well . . . as a rock!' He grinned. 'The same goes for the soundings we took inside the cave. You'll always be able to hear the sea from your basement, but it isn't a threat. OK?' Josh paused, then straightened up and began to fold up the papers. I had the impression he was in a hurry to leave, and knew why, of course.

'Whew! What a relief!' Carol's anxious face cleared and she raised a hand to her head. 'Secretly I've been so worried for you all.'

'I must go and phone Rob, on his mobile, right away . . . ' Claire jumped up and ran from the room.

'And I must go, too.' Josh picked up his briefcase and turned to leave. 'Mike's waiting outside for me.'

'Of course. Good luck with what you find.'

He looked over his shoulder and our eyes met.

'And Josh, thank you. Thank you so much.'

He nodded and raised a hand. 'See you later. And I'll tell you all about it then.'

★　★　★

'I'm glad now that we didn't ask the residents to leave.' I turned to Alex who was perched on the corner of the table, one leg swinging. She nodded and said something I didn't catch.

However, I had postponed further bookings, until we were absolutely sure. But we were over the height of the season and they were beginning to tail off anyway, so all in all it could have been a whole lot worse.

Now all the jubilation was over however, I had come down to earth with a bump.

'Of course,' I said as we both moved to leave the room. 'We're not out of the wood yet, don't forget. The house surveyor is coming tomorrow.'

14

The structural surveyor turned up promptly next day as arranged and set to work. He too used a hand-held electronic device, which was apparently a wall penetrating radar.

We were all on edge while he was in the house, not able to settle to anything as he was all over the place. Rob had taken a half-day off to go around with him, and there was nothing the rest of us could do but wait.

I drifted out to the garden, where Alex was sitting at the picnic table, watching Isobel tossing a ball for Jess to catch. Over the past few days the countryside had subtly begun its change from the brightness of high summer to the more subdued tints of approaching autumn. Although the middle part of the day was still warm and balmy, there was also a nip in the air in the mornings and evenings that spoke of cooler days to come.

I'd noticed lately that Alex was reluctant to let Isobel out of her sight since the accident, which was totally understandable, although she was looking bored stiff. But her face lit up with a smile as she saw me coming across the grass, and she patted the bench beside her.

'Hi, Mel, I'm really glad to see you. I've been dying for a bit of company, but I don't want to leave Iz on her own.' I sat down and leaned my elbows on the table.

'How's the surveyor getting on indoors?' Alex jerked her head in the direction of the house.

'Pretty well, as far as I know. Rob's taken him down to the cellar, and after that I think he might be through.'

'But you won't get the results for a day or two, I suppose, will you?' Alex twisted in her seat and put her feet up on the bench, hugging her knees.

I shook my head. 'No. The waiting is

the worst part. Although I did tell him we want to know as soon as possible, as we have the residents to think of. He seems to be an obliging sort of chap, so maybe he'll hurry it up if he can.'

Alex absently ran her fingers through her dark crop, her eyes on her small daughter who was now rolling on the ground with the dog, shrieking with laughter as they tussled with the ball.

'I shall have to think about going home pretty soon, Mel.' Alex glanced over her shoulder at me. 'Andy's due back at the end of the month. And Izzy starts school soon, too.'

'I suppose you must. How the weeks have flown.' I thought back to the beginning of the season. 'It doesn't seem that long since you came.'

And Josh as well, of course. My mind went back to our original meeting, when he and Chris had arrived so unexpectedly out of the storm, blown to us on the wings of the wind. And now with summer's end and the end too of his job, Josh would soon be going back to his normal life. And leaving me behind.

I sighed, then covered it with a smile. 'It's because we've been so busy, of course. It's been lovely having your help.'

Alex shrugged. 'I've enjoyed it.' Then her eyes twinkled. 'In spite of all the drama that I never expected.'

I nodded. 'Gosh, no! None of us could possibly have seen that lot coming. What with the slip, then Isobel, then Josh. We've had more drama in a few weeks than most people experience in a lifetime.'

Alex's face clouded. 'I feel I've aged ten years since Isobel . . . ' Her gaze followed the little girl's running feet.

I nodded. 'And for her the whole thing was over and forgotten in a few hours.'

'Well, that's children for you.' Alex shrugged. 'And as for saying she hadn't disobeyed me and gone over there on her own, I suppose to a child that age it was perfectly logical. With Jess, she wasn't on her own.'

I smiled. 'Yes, Izzy treats that dog as if she were human. Of course, she never realised the danger she was in at all.'

I rose to my feet and sighed. 'But this worry over the house is still hovering over us.' I turned away. 'I'd better go in Alex, and see if they've finished. I can't settle anywhere until he's gone.'

As I crossed the grass however, the two of them came out of the side door; Rob was obviously seeing the surveyor out. As the man reached his car Rob raised a hand, then came towards us looking serious.

'How was it?' I said eagerly. 'Did he tell you anything?'

Rob rasped a hand over his chin and shrugged. 'Not really. He was very cagey. Didn't say much at all, in fact. He's one of those men of few words. But he did promise to put his report in the post as soon as he possibly can.' I nodded. So we had to go on waiting for a while longer yet.

⋆   ⋆   ⋆

I was just about to go inside when the truck came zooming in and screeched to a halt in the yard. Josh and Mike jumped out, talking animatedly to each other, and there was such an air of excitement that curiosity stopped me in my tracks.

'Mel,' Josh called out as they both came towards me. 'It's good news!' His face was transformed from the moody and morose character I'd glimpsed more and more often lately. Now a huge grin spread over his features, and there was a spring in his step I hadn't seen for a long time. At his side Mike looked equally jubilant.

Now I realised why, and didn't need to ask them. 'You've found it, then? It was the adit?'

'Yes!' Josh punched the air. 'Just where I knew it had to be all along.'

'Wonderful! Congratulations.' My smile was as wide as his, but tinged with melancholy too. For this find only

254

emphasised the fact that Josh would be leaving soon. And it was highly unlikely I would ever see him again.

'We had another quick look in the cave too, while we were there,' Mike put in, 'and we want to explore that further. Only Josh is desperate to get his report sent off first. You know how little time we've got left.'

I nodded. 'Yes. Josh told me.' It seemed ages ago that he'd taken me into his confidence that day, when he had been so down. When he had called me a good listener.

'We're going back as soon as Josh has sent in his report,' Mike finished, with a jerk of his thumb towards the direction they'd just come from.

'I'll phone them first, though, and make sure they hear the news as soon as possible.' Josh's eyes sparkled. 'Maybe that landslip had a silver lining after all, in a way, in spite of all the trouble it has caused.'

His smile faded as he absently fingered the place on his head where the wound had been.

'Because,' he brightened again, 'if it hadn't been for that we'd never have found the adit. And as the ground had to be checked for stability too, that's saved the firm from having to do it. Now there's nothing to stop them bringing in heavy machinery to de-water the mine, whenever they want to start.'

'Will you be staying on to see that happen?' A forlorn hope, but I had to ask.

Both of us were solemn-faced as our eyes met. Josh shook his head. 'Oh, no, Mel. My part in all this is finished now. I shall be on tenterhooks though, until I know for certain if we've secured the job for Cornwall, and I shall hang around until then.' He smiled.

'Apart from which, I'm curious to know how big this new centre's going to be, and how it's going to impinge on the mining work, if we do get the contract.' He shrugged broad shoulders. 'After that, I'm entitled to a short break, then it'll be on to the next assignment.'

'So, in the meantime,' Mike said, 'we thought we'd have a thorough look at that cave. Right, mate?' He nudged Josh with an elbow and sauntered off towards the truck.

'Right.' Josh nodded, raised a hand to me and was about to follow Mike when Alex and Isobel came hurrying up the garden, obviously coming to see what all the fuss was about.

Isobel came racing on ahead and clutched at Josh's hand. 'Come and play ball, Josh, please, please?'

'Hello, young lady.' He casually dropped his hard hat on to her head, completely obscuring her vision, then rapped his knuckles on the top. 'Anybody home in there?'

Isobel burst into delighted squeals of laughter as she wriggled out from under it.

'Sorry mate,' he said as he retrieved the hat. 'Another time. Right now there is work to be done.' He turned and called back over his shoulder. 'Mel will fill you in with the news, Alex. I'm going into Penzance to send in this report straight away. I'll see you all later.'

★   ★   ★

I didn't see Josh any more that day. It must have been the early hours before he came in, as we all stayed up to watch a film and I was later going to bed than usual. Presumably he and the others had stopped at a pub in Penzance before coming back. Hopefully to celebrate, if they had succeeded in getting the contract for Cornwall.

I caught a glimpse of him mid-morning, going off with Mike and Jim in the truck, presumably to explore the cave, but that was all. Partway through the afternoon however, we had a phone call which drove all other thoughts out of my head.

I'd been stacking some stuff in the office when I heard Claire come running down the passage, calling my name.

'Oh, Mel, there you are!' She stopped abruptly. 'Didn't you hear the phone?'

'No, I had the door shut. What is it?' I turned and faced her, taking in for the first time her flushed cheeks and sparkling eyes.

'It was from the surveyor's office.' She clutched my arm and shook it.

'Already?' I gaped at her for a moment as the penny dropped. 'But we didn't expect to hear from them for days! Wh — what did they say?'

But I could see, I didn't have to ask. Claire was almost dancing up and down with glee, and her beaming smile was lighting up the tiny room.

'It's all OK!' She seized my other arm and whirled me round. 'We're in the clear. There's no structural damage, Mel. He didn't find a thing wrong. Not a crack anywhere. The old house is solid as a rock!'

'Oh, Claire!' I sank down onto the chair, my head reeling. And not only with being twirled around. It was just too much to take in. We'd spent so long wondering, waiting, hoping, but nevertheless planning for the worst, that the relief had left me physically shaking.

'You are sure, aren't you?' I was gaping at her like an idiot. 'Only . . . I can hardly believe it.'

'You have to believe it!' She grabbed my hands and pulled me to my feet, enveloping me in an enormous hug. 'They're going to put written proof in the post, but knowing how anxious we were, they phoned first. Wasn't that good of them?' She released me and gave a little skip. 'Now let's go find the others and spread the good news.'

Before we had a chance to do so however, Rob came bursting in obviously full of excitement as well, waving the local paper in one hand, with a bottle of what looked like champagne under his other arm.

'Hey girls, look at this!' He flourished the paper under our noses, open at a headline I could read from where I was standing.

Development of proposed visitor centre at Carn Dhu called off after large landslips in the area. Too great a risk of further coastal erosion to make the project viable.

'Wh . . . what? Called off?' Claire turned to me in astonishment 'Oh, wow!'

'What — permanently? Are you sure? Show me.' I pulled the paper out of Rob's grasp and Claire and I scanned it together.

'It's true! It's true! The company's pulled out altogether! They're going to build it somewhere else. Oh, fantastic!' Claire grabbed my arms and we did a little dance around the room while Rob looked indulgently on.

'Time for celebrations I think.' Rob pulled another bottle out of his jacket pocket. 'It's a lovely evening. How about having a barbie in the garden?'

'Perfect! Great idea.' I nodded, suddenly spurred into activity. 'Let's go and forage in the kitchen, Claire, and see what we can find to eat.'

★ ★ ★

Rob had just got the barbecue going and the sausages and burgers sizzling over it, when Josh and Mike appeared in the truck and parked at the side of the house.

Josh gave a wave and came towards us over the grass, a wide smile on his face.

'Wow, that's looking good! We could smell it way over there as we were coming back.' He pointed a finger.

'Well, there's loads of stuff here. Plenty for everybody. Why don't you both join us? We're celebrating.' I leaned back in the canvas chair I was lounging in, and put down my glass as I told him the latest news.

'Brilliant! Oh, I'm so glad for you, that's absolutely wonderful! And well . . . about staying for the barbie . . . I didn't mean . . . I hope you don't think I was hinting . . . ' Josh looked discomfited and his cheeks coloured slightly.

'Of course not,' Rob boomed. 'You're very welcome. I'm outnumbered here by all these females.' He flourished a long-handled cooking fork in the air. 'You'll even up the sides. Take a seat and pour yourself a drink. This is nearly ready.'

'Well, if you're sure, that'll be great. Thanks very much.' Josh grinned and stretched himself out on the grass beside me.

'Yeah. Thanks Rob, old mate.' Mike sat down at the picnic bench. 'I'm starving. We've been climbing up and down that cliff all day.'

'And apart from making a final check on the adit, you'll never guess what else we found.' Josh sat up, his eyes betraying his suppressed excitement as with a nod of thanks to Rob, he accepted a burger in a bun.

'Oh? What was that?' We all turned to him with interest.

'Well,' Josh waved the bun as he spoke. 'We went right into the back of the cave, as far as we could, I thought.

But when we got there, we found there was this hidden passage leading off from one side. We couldn't see it until we turned the corner.'

'So we started crawling up it,' Mike took up the story, 'and took a torch, not knowing what we might find. It was narrow, too low to stand up in mostly, but not blocked or anything.'

Josh took a huge bite of his bun and spoke through it. 'I kept testing the walls and the roof for stability as we went along, but it was firm and solid all the way. Damp of course, and dripping water down our necks, but sandy underfoot.'

'How exciting! It sounds like something out of an adventure story!' And so dangerous too, I thought, shivering as I imagined both men buried underneath another sudden rock fall with no chance of a rescue party turning up this time. I glanced down at the curly head so close to me and felt a fresh stab of pain. I could have lost him forever. Even the thought of him going out of my life in the near future was better than that.

'Where did the passage go? Did you ever find the end of it?' Alex's gaze was riveted on Josh's face and she seemed to have forgotten the sausage speared on her fork.

'Well, it wound on and on for so long I began to wonder if it had an end. I was worrried, because if we didn't find it, no-one would ever know where we were.'

'The first rule of caving,' Alex chipped in, 'is always tell someone where you're going, and roughly how long you're going to be.'

'I know.' Josh nodded. 'But we'd no idea what we were getting into. Anyway, we couldn't go back because the passage in some places was too narrow to turn round in. It was quite claustrophobic at the tightest parts.' He shrugged. 'And we had to scramble over several fallen rocks. Not for the fainthearted at all.' He laughed to lighten the tension.

'Anyway, we pushed on.' Mike drained his glass and took up his fork. 'All I could see was Josh's rear and the pinprick of torchlight in front of him. But eventually we actually saw a gleam of daylight.'

'Oh, the relief! I've never been so glad to see anything in all my life.' Josh grinned. 'Just as I was, I admit, getting a bit anxious. But even then, it wasn't easy getting out. We followed the light up a steep climb to the outside, but then we still had to hack our way through all this vegetation.' He waved his arm about descriptively.

'Brambles and gorse, great clumps of ivy, heather and stuff, had all grown over the gap and filled it in. Then when we did eventually emerge all we could do was collapse, exhausted at the top.'

Mike chuckled, reliving the moment. 'We just lay there flat on our backs like stranded fish, both of us gasping for air. That's why we're so filthy.' He looked a little embarrassed now as he glanced down at his stained sweat-shirt and ragged jeans.

'And where were you?' Rob put down his serving tool and waved away the drifting smoke from his red face.

'That's what is so fascinating.' Josh's face was alight with excitement. 'We found that the passage was only partly formed by nature. It led into the ruins of Wheal Hope. And that hole we pushed up through was the entrance to an abandoned shaft.'

'Really?' We all stared at him with renewed interest.

Josh nodded. 'And that's not all.' He paused and looked around at us. 'The rest of it you'll never believe.'

15

As the rest of us stared at him transfixed, Josh pushed aside his paper plate and straightened up, placing his forearms on his knees.

'What I didn't tell you was, when we were coming up the tunnel I happened to shine the torch upwards at one point. And there in the roof I could see what looked like a great seam of copper-bearing ore. Then when I swung the light to and fro I was pretty sure it ran most of the way along the passage.'

'It's never been worked,' Mike added. 'Looks like the shaft was sunk from up the top, halted at a bend when they met the natural tunnel coming up from the beach, and for some reason the ore was never extracted. By today's prices it would be worth a small fortune.'

'And it's all there, just waiting to be brought out!' Josh waved his hands in excitement. 'Do you see what this will mean to the company that gets the contract? Half the work is already done. All they have to do is come along and pick the stuff out. And make a huge profit almost immediately.'

'How amazing!' My gaze fixed on Josh's face as I tried to take it all in.

'It certainly is.' Josh rose to his feet. 'And I need to phone my firm and tell them all this, right away. As well as have a shower and a change of clothes.' He laughed, brushing himself down. He glanced at his watch before adding, 'I shall have to leave a message of course, but at least they'll get the news first thing in the morning. It should give them that extra little push to give the contract to Cornwall. I hope!'

'We'll keep our fingers crossed,' I replied as he hurried off towards the house.

'Thanks a lot for supper,' Josh called over his shoulder as the rest of us, replete and too lazy to move, sat around talking and enjoying the calm of the evening.

Mike was the first to move. 'Well, if you'll excuse me,' he said, rising to his feet, 'I'd better get that truck back before they lock up the yard. And I'm for a shower too, after all the scrabbling about in that tunnel.' He took off the broad-brimmed hat that he was never without, and ran a hand through his bushy mane of hair.

'Where are you staying, Mike?' Rob inquired. 'B&B in Penzance, is it?'

He'd put into words what I'd been wondering; why Mike hadn't stayed here with us as Josh did. But then I understood.

The big man chuckled.

'No, not me, mate. I've got my trusty camper van parked up on a site above the town. All mod cons and a fantastic view over Mount's Bay and the castle.' He replaced the hat and waved a hand as he strode off. 'Thanks a lot for the grub. Much appreciated. See you.'

Soon after that we stirred ourselves and began to pack up the remains of the barbecue.

'That was a great idea of yours Rob,' I remarked as he started to clear out the ashes. 'I think we all enjoyed having the cooking done for us for once.'

'Oh, I get great ideas like that all the time,' he joked, 'but mostly I'm not appreciated!' And he wiped a blackened hand over his already grimy face.

★   ★   ★

A couple of days later, Alex announced that it was time for her and Isobel to leave.

'Izzy's absolutely loved it down here, Mel, and so have I. We've had a wonderful summer, in spite of everything!'

I joined in her laughter. It was so easy to laugh these days. I hadn't realised how much the doom and gloom had been getting to me until it was all over. Now the only cloud in the sky was my personal one, and it seemed more unlikely than ever that it would have a silver lining.

'We're going to miss you so much,' I replied. 'It'll be quiet without Izzy running about, and her chatter. But of course you have to get back to your own life again. And Alex,' I touched her arm, 'thanks for all the help you've given us.'

'It was nothing. I enjoyed it.' Alex waved a dismissive hand. 'Now, what I thought I'd do is pop over and say goodbye to Mum this afternoon, and then get the early train tomorrow morning.'

★   ★   ★

After the bustle of getting Alex and Isobel packed up and on to the train home, Claire and I turned our attention to winding down the business of the hostel. It had been, in spite of all the ups and downs, a very successful season. And another reason for the cheerful mood everyone seemed to be in.

Having been indoors for most of the day, stocktaking and clearing up, by early evening I was longing for some fresh air and a leisurely walk.

I looked out of the window at the familiar scene. The sun had just begun its gradual descent into the western sea and there wasn't a breath of wind.

A couple of gulls, silhouetted against the light, flapped lazily into the distance and disappeared. In the other direction Carn Dhu, living up to its name of black earn, was already shrouded in shadow and mystery.

When Jess saw me putting on my jacket and hopefully pricked up her ears, I seized her lead from its peg and took her with me.

I paused to open the gate, intending to head for the carn and enjoy the view and the clear air from up there, when a soft voice came from behind me.

'Are you off for a walk, Mel? Do you mind if I join you?'

'Josh! I didn't hear you coming. Yes, I need to stretch my legs and Jess hasn't been out much today.' I turned to smile at him. 'Of course I don't mind. I'll be glad of your company.'

If only I could tell him how glad. But it seemed we were destined to part with nothing resolved between us. Josh it seemed was oblivious to my feelings for him, and didn't return them. Bolder women than I, Sam for example, might have dropped a few hints, but that was not my style. Better he should never know than risk humiliation on that scale.

'I thought I might go up the carn,' I said with a smile. 'Is that OK for you?'

'Perfect.' We fell into an easy stride, side by side at first, over the open ground leading towards the hill.

'Have you heard yet whether you've got the contract for opening the mine?' I looked up into his familiar face, almost drinking in the features so I could remember them in the lonely times ahead when he would be gone.

'Yes. And I wanted you to be the first to know, Mel. That's why, when I saw you going out, it seemed a good chance to get you on your own.' He paused, his eyes sparkling. 'They've given the contract to Cornwall!'

'Oh, that's marvellous. Fantastic news! Well done!' My natural response to anyone else in that position would be to throw my arms around them in a hug of congratulation and shared excitement. However, I had to forcibly keep my hands at my sides as I faced the love of my life, so near and yet so far away, our bodies almost touching and the air crackling with words unsaid.

'I'm so pleased for you,' I said inadequately. It sounded pathetic, but without telling him what was really in my heart, what else could I say?

'So we shall soon have developers taking over Wheal Hope.' Having just got rid of the proposed visitor centre, I was wondering instead what this was going to mean in terms of our privacy, and our business.

Josh must have read my mind and picked up on my mixed feelings. 'You will.' He paused in his stride and turned to meet my eyes.

'But Mel, they'll be far enough away not to disturb you. Right across the moor. Really. And I'm sure it will bring you extra business, too. Think about it, the workers will have to lodge somewhere, and having a hostel right here couldn't be more convenient, could it? Nothing like the upheaval the visitors' centre development would have caused. So it won't be too bad.'

'I suppose so. I hadn't thought of that.' I smiled. Put like that it did seem more reassuring.

We walked on in companionable silence for a few yards, one behind the other while Jess scampered on ahead, each of us seeming lost in our own thoughts, before Josh stopped again and I almost bumped into him.

'There's something else I must tell you, Mel, too. Something I thought out in bed, when I couldn't sleep. The night after we'd found the passageway.'

'Oh, yes? What's that, then?'

'Well,' we walked slowly on as he spoke, 'I was thinking about the old legend of Kit's cavern and his supposed treasure, you know?'

I nodded. 'Mmm. What about it?'

'Well, it occurred to me that Kit could possibly have been a miner for his day job, and a smuggler on the side.'

'A miner?' I gave him a blank look.

Josh nodded. 'It would account for two things, you see. One,' he held up a finger, 'the cave would have been perfect for bringing in his goods from a boat, and storing them. They could have stayed there indefinitely somewhere above the high water line. That is, until he had a chance to bring them up the passage to the top of the shaft and hide them again in the undergrowth, or distribute them to his customers.'

I felt my eyes light up as I turned to him in astonishment. 'Oh, yes. That would have worked. So you believe there's something in the legend, then?'

'Who knows?' Josh shrugged. 'I'm only guessing how it could have been.'

'But you said two things,' I reminded him. 'What was the other one?'

'Oh, yes.' He raised another finger. 'As we said, the lode running up through the tunnel is worth a fortune in terms of mineral wealth. My guess is that copper was Kit's real treasure.' Josh turned towards me, his face animated and his hands gesturing as he spoke.

'If he was the only one who knew about it, and if he was a miner, he could well have been waiting until he'd finished with his smuggling runs and could 'discover' the lode in the course of his work.'

'Oh, wow, yes!' I felt my face light up with enthusiasm. 'And another thing. If he was a 'tributer' — you know, a miner who staked a claim for what he thought was a good pitch — and he knew what it was worth, he'd be on to a good thing. It would have made him a wealthy man.' I arched my brows as our glances met. 'I wonder why he didn't? I'd love to know.'

'So would I, but we never shall.' Josh

paused to step round Jess's rump as the dog explored a rabbit-hole, tail quivering. 'Maybe he was caught by the revenue men and jailed for his activities, maybe he even died before he could get at the ore. Miners did die young in the past. But there must have been rumours going around about his activities at the time, for the legend to have taken hold.'

I nodded. 'That's true. Anyway, I'm really glad Kit didn't mine that seam, else it wouldn't have been there for you to find!'

Josh looked solemnly back at me. 'You know Mel, in a strange way that landslip, instead of being a near-tragedy, has turned out to be the key to everything good that's happened since. Without it we would never have found the adit, or the 'treasure', and the contract would have gone to the Mexican firm for certain.'

'And we would have had contractors building almost on our doorstep too,' I added.

The track was growing narrower and more stony now as we reached the lower slopes, and we had to walk in single file. Josh went ahead, his long legs swallowing up the sharply-rising path, while I had to keep my head down and watch where I was putting my feet.

After a while, he stopped and sat down on a flat boulder, waiting for me to catch up.

'So what kept you?' he joked, as I puffed up the last and steepest bit and sat down at his side.

'It's all right for you, daddy-long-legs,' I elbowed him playfully in the ribs. 'I can't help being a shortle.'

'And there's nothing wrong with being 'vertically challenged', as they call it now, don't they?' Josh looked me up and down. 'In fact, perched on that rock in your red coat you look just like a Cornish pixie on a toadstool. All you need is the pointy hat!'

'Oh . . . you . . . ' I laughed, wishing

it could always be like this, the easy banter, the jokes.

'And talking of long legs,' I shifted more comfortably on my 'toadstool', 'Sam told me you used to be a champion runner. I could certainly believe it that day when you went sprinting off after Isobel.'

'Oh, yes. That was all a long time ago.' Josh had sobered and his gaze was far away over the valley. The hostel looked like a doll's house from up here, dwarfed by the immensity of the landscape. If it hadn't been for the pinpricks of a couple of lighted windows, it might not have existed at all.

'Why didn't you keep it up?' I asked, genuinely interested. I still knew so little of his past.

'Oh,' Josh lifted his shoulders in a shrug, 'it was the pressure, Mel. The pressure always to do more — to do better, and then better still. In the end I snapped under the strain and was ill for several months.'

He paused and sighed. 'While I was out of action I did a lot of thinking. And I decided I'd had enough — that I was going back to my original career. The fame and adulation had been pumping the adrenaline and keeping me going up to then. But I'd lost the urge to keep pushing myself.'

His face darkened and he looked down at the hands lying in his lap.

'There had been a . . . girl, too,' he added softly, 'but she dropped me when I backed out. I can see now just how shallow she was. But at the time . . . ' he raised his head and our eyes met, 'I thought she loved me Mel, loved me for myself, not the public figure I'd become. And that hurt. It took me a long time to accept it.'

He drew in a deep breath. 'Then when I came out of hospital I found nobody had missed me much. The world had moved on. Plus I was no longer fit. I'd put on weight and inches lying about and it was too much effort to face working myself back up, you know what I mean?' He turned his head and I nodded.

'So I shook myself out of the self-pity and went back to university. After belatedly picking up where I left off I gained my qualifications and went abroad to work. After a few years I found the job I'm doing now.'

'And you're happy?' I don't know what made me say that, it seemed to come out of nowhere.

Josh turned his head sharply. 'Happy?' He raised an eyebrow. 'As happy as most people, I suppose.'

It was an enigmatic answer. 'And how about you, Mel?' He neatly turned it round. 'Are you happy?'

How to answer that one. 'About the same as most people,' I echoed, batting it back, and he smiled.

'And I suppose you'll be going up to London soon, to see your friend. You did say you would at the end of the season, didn't you?'

And he'd remembered that; how strange. The remark was a casual one, but Josh was still looking intently at me as he spoke. 'Is that the chap in the suit I saw you with that day when he called at the hostel?'

I frowned, momentarily puzzled.

'Oh, no.' I shook my head. 'That was David.'

Josh gave me a look I couldn't interpret and the smile vanished from his face.

Jess came to lay her head in my lap, silently pleading to get walking again as she was bored. I stroked her soft nose, then stirred and rose to my feet.

'Josh, I'm getting stiff with sitting on this stone, and Jess wants to be on the move too. So shall we go on?'

'OK,' Josh muttered. His tone was curt and I didn't catch the rest, as Jess began to bark with relief and was capering round our feet as we moved off.

A slightly uncomfortable silence I couldn't account for fell as we took the level track across the top of the hill. But it was getting dark now and we needed to concentrate on where we were walking. In places, tough roots of bracken and heather formed loops across the track, lurking to catch the unwary toe.

At the back of my mind I was thinking about what Josh had said about the legend. Kit was supposed to haunt this hill, and if anyone believed in ghosts, this would be the place to be haunted. In the twilight and stillness, both rocks and bushes took on eerie, unnatural shapes and cast strange shadows. I shivered. It was not a place to come alone after dark.

At a turn in the path, there was a towering crag that we had to skirt around, and I had just paused to ease my way round it, when it happened.

My heart gave an almighty leap and I froze as without warning, a ghostly figure reared up out of the night directly in front of me. A huge shape, white and silent, its arms spread wide like the ghost of all my childhood imaginings, while out of its round, staring face two black eyes hovered inches in front of me, and it gave a low moan.

I panicked, screaming over and over, falling to my knees as I dived for cover into a stand of scrubby bushes. Anywhere out of the way of that ghastly thing which was now swooping over and around me.

I felt the wind of its passing, and stayed huddled, gibbering like an idiot. Josh who had been a few paces further on around the tall crag, now came running back to me.

'Mel, whatever's the matter? Are you hurt?' His anxious eyes peered closely down to me as he lifted me to my feet as I gasped for breath. He kept his arms around me, warm and comforting, as my heartbeat steadied and I tried to speak. But my voice trembled and I fell against him sobbing, clutching at his jacket to keep myself upright.

'Oh, Josh, I was so frightened,' I babbled, ' . . . there was this th-thing . . . I saw a ghost . . . and I've never believed in . . . '

'Hush now.' Keeping both arms around me, he drew me down to sit beside him on the ground.

'D — did you see it?' I stammered. 'It was just before you got here.' Shaking, I turned my tear-filled eyes up to meet his.

'Er . . . ' Josh paused and cleared his throat. 'Well, yes. I saw it, Mel.'

'You did?' Shock instantly quietened my sobs and I felt my jaw drop. 'And . . . and . . . you're not scared?'

Josh shook his head and I saw the corners of his mouth lift. 'No, it didn't scare me a bit.' He paused and I could swear his eyes were twinkling. 'Mel, it was only an owl.'

'An owl?' I gaped at him. 'But . . . it couldn't have been. It was nothing like an owl! It was white . . . and big . . . and horrible.'

Josh nodded. 'It was a barn owl.' He spread his hands and shrugged. 'I should have thought, living here all your life, you would have realised . . . '

A harmless little barn owl. I clapped one hand to my mouth. Oh no, what a fool I'd made of myself! I felt colour rise to my cheeks and was thankful for the darkness, but had a sneaking suspicion that in spite of it Josh knew exactly how I was feeling.

'But you're shaking all over.' Only as his arms tightened did I realise that my head was resting on his shoulder as if it was the most natural place in the world for it to be.

16

I was in no hurry to recover from my fright, and prolonged the moment I spent in Josh's arms for as long as I decently could. Over his shoulder I could see a full moon was rising now, etching the crags in bold relief, and threading fingers of silver towards us over the turf.

I sighed. It was a night just made for romance. And here I was, wrapped in the arms of the man I loved most in the world, and he was making no further move towards me. I slipped out of his embrace, no longer wanting to make it last.

'Are you sure you're all right now, Mel?' Josh looked at me in concern as I suddenly drew away.

'Of course I am.' My nerves were wound so tight with frustration I couldn't help snapping at him. Why couldn't he feel as I did? Was there something wrong with me that I was so unattractive to him? I drew in a deep breath. 'Thank you,' I added politely. 'As you said, it was only a harmless bird.'

* * *

A few days later when I was in the kitchen doing a load of ironing, Josh put his head around the door.

'Hi, Mel, can I have a word? Shan't keep you more than a minute or so.'

'Of course.' I bent to switch off the iron. 'Come on in. Cup of coffee? I'm just about to have one.'

'Thanks, but no thanks. I only dropped in to tell you that I'm going away.'

My heart sank. Was he going back home? To pick up the threads of his life again? But of course he was. It made complete sense. His work here was finished, he'd been living away for the best part of six months. What else did I expect? But suddenly I felt a weight like a cold and heavy stone settle deep inside me, as reality dawned. I would never see him again.

'There's some business I have to see to. I don't know quite how long it'll take. Probably a week to ten days.' Josh lifted his shoulders and spread his hands. 'But I was wondering, if you don't mind, whether I could leave some of my stuff here temporarily, and pick it up again when I get back. It's only a couple of boxes. If I could stow them in the office where they wouldn't be in your way, would that be OK?'

'Of course it would. No problem at all.'

I raised my head and forced a smile to my face as our glances met.

'Oh, thanks, Mel.' He grinned broadly and ran a hand over his hair. 'That would be great. I'll go and fetch that stuff from the car now.'

* * *

291

Josh's departure left me feeling as if the light had gone out of my life. Having had him around for so long I'd grown used to feeding on his smile, his nearness, the chats and jokes we had shared. Of him just being there.

But now, with winter approaching, the dark evenings setting in seemed to echo the darkness in my soul. I must have moped around the house like a ghost of myself, although none of the others appeared to notice.

This won't do, I told myself sternly as I caught sight of my pale face in the mirror one morning. *Josh never was going to be yours and never will be. So get over it. Take a grip on yourself and get a life, for goodness sake.*

So I decided I would take Sam up on her invitation and go to London for a few days. It would be a complete break and would be just the thing to take me out of myself. But, a small voice in my head persisted. *What if Josh should come back for his belongings while you're away and you missed him?* I silenced the voice and went to phone Sam before I changed my mind.

★ ★ ★

I was in my room, daydreaming as I packed my clothes into a small case, when someone knocked on the door.

'Mel, are you in there?' came Claire's gentle voice.

'Yes, I am. Come in,' I replied, without looking up from the clothes I'd heaped on the bed.

She closed the door and must have been standing with her back to it, waiting for me to turn round, for she didn't come forward into the room.

'Mel,' she said, and something in the tone of her voice made me turn round and glance at her. Then I saw the excitement on her face and the sparkle in her eyes.

'What's up with you? Won the lottery or something?' I joked.

'Better, much better,' she whispered, coming forward to clutch my arm. 'The best news ever, in fact.'

Then the penny dropped and my heart began to thump. 'Claire!' I jumped up and gave her my full attention. 'You're not . . . it isn't . . . ?'

She nodded happily, with tears standing in her eyes as well. 'It's a baby, Mel. Truly. I just can't believe it!' She was shaking her head as she placed her hands on her stomach in wonder.

'Oh, Claire!' I threw both arms around her and drew her down to sit on the bed beside me. 'At last! How marvellous! And you are quite sure?' Our eyes met and she nodded.

'I waited until the doctor was certain. Because after last time, I hardly dared let myself get excited, you know?' She bit her lip and her expression became more serious.

'And how are you feeling? Really, I mean.' I looked at her with concern.

'Absolutely wonderful. I'm hardly even getting sick in the mornings. Not a bit like before. I'm sure it's going to be OK. I feel different, Mel. Quite different from that other awful time.'

'Oh, I'm so glad for you. I can't tell you how glad.' I squeezed her arm. 'And Rob? I suppose he's thrilled to bits, too.'

Claire laughed. 'I'll say. He's like a dog with two tails. But he will nag at me. Don't do this, don't do that. Take care. And he won't let me lift anything heavier than a paper bag.' She arched her brows. 'If it was up to him I'd spend the whole nine months in bed!'

'It's only natural for him to worry,' I smiled with her. 'Like you, he's thinking back to last time. What fun though, to have a tiny infant in the house! When is your due date, Claire?'

'Early April, they think.'

'A spring baby, fantastic!' I hugged her again and we drifted into a happy discussion of the endless equipment we were going to need for this tiny new arrival.

$$\star \quad \star \quad \star$$

Thrilled as I was by Claire's news, it only emphasised even more how empty my own personal life was, so I set off for London as soon as Sam could have me.

She had a small flat in Blackheath, with a pleasant view over the grassy heath and the church to the tall trees of Greenwich Park. It was an attractive, semi-rural situation while still being only a short train ride from the city.

'I'm so glad you managed to tear yourself away at last, Mel.' We were strolling arm in arm through the park towards the observatory one evening. 'I never thought you'd actually make it.' She looked closely into my face. 'At least, as long as Josh Stephens was still down there with you.'

I was watching a squirrel run chattering up a huge horse chestnut tree. 'Oh, dear, was it that obvious? I had no idea.' I lowered my head, avoiding her gaze, and kicked at some early fallen leaves.

'Only because I know you so well.'

Sam chuckled. 'I can read between the lines. Has he finished the work he was doing there yet?'

'Yes. Oh, yes. He found what he was looking for. Now he's gone off somewhere. I don't know where.' I shrugged. 'I imagine to see about the next job. He's left a few things to pick up later, but I don't suppose I shall ever see him again.'

I tried to appear nonchalant but Sam who, as she'd said, could read me like a book, wasn't fooled. She fixed me with a steely look.

'And you mind, don't you?' Miserably, unable to hide from her laser-like stare, I nodded.

'Well, for goodness sake, Mel Treloar,' she burst out, 'why haven't you dropped him a hint or two? All this time Josh has been staying under your roof and you haven't made a move? I would have, long before now!'

'Sam, I know you would.' I placed a hand on her sleeve. 'But we're two different people.' Fired up now, I was going to have my say.

'I'm no shrinking violet, but I can tell you, we've been in certain situations where Josh could have made some sign if he was interested — where there was an obvious opening. But he never has, so he just doesn't want to. Simple. He had one disastrous love affair — you told me that yourself. Perhaps that put him off all women.'

'Pooh, one affair and it puts him off for life? I don't believe it!' Sam snorted. I recalled her 'pebbles on the beach' attitude to men and didn't expect her to understand.

'Well, I'm certainly not going to throw myself at him, if that's what you think.' I glared at her. 'I do have some pride.'

I turned to stare with tear-dimmed eyes at the statue of General Wolfe perched on his lofty pedestal looking out over the Thames, and sniffed.

As my eyes cleared though, I realised what a viewpoint this actually was and it took me out of myself for a moment.

It was one of those clear, still evenings with hardly any breeze, and I realised I could see right across the river as far as Greenwich College and the Isle of Dogs on the far bank. To the west I could even make out the distant dome of St Paul's.

But Sam hadn't finished with me yet. Unperturbed by my outburst, she gave me a long and calculating look.

'When did Josh say he was coming back to pick up his things?' she asked.

'Um, in about a week, I think he said. Maybe ten days.'

'Well, as soon as this weekend is over and you get back to Cornwall, make sure you do something, do you hear me? Nothing ventured, nothing gained,' she urged. 'I can't believe he can be as indifferent to an attractive girl like you, as you say he is, Mel.'

Sam walked on a few steps, thinking and talking to me over her shoulder. 'No, there must be something in the way, blocking him.' She spun round. 'So, get in there and find out what it is.'

'Oh, Sam.' I laughed helplessly in spite of myself. 'You make it sound so easy!'

'You've nothing to lose,' she stated firmly. 'It's a case of action on your part or let him go out of your life forever. The choice is yours.'

★　★　★

Sam's words echoed in my mind all through the long journey home from Paddington. From her point of view what she said was all well and good, but how on earth could I possibly approach Josh like that? What would I say? How could I put to him the fact that I loved him more than I'd ever thought possible? I couldn't drop hints about something so stupendous. And run the risk of rejection and ridicule? I just couldn't do it.

I sat hunched in my corner, leafing through a magazine and taking in none of it, while my thoughts whirled in endless confusion.

At one point I dozed off and awoke as we entered a station to find I had a worse headache than before.

However, I'd really enjoyed the break, which had temporarily shaken me out of my narrow confines. Sam's company and constant chatter had been like a breath of fresh air, even though my problems were still unsolved.

*   *   *

I didn't have to wait long for Josh's return. Just two days later I was gazing out of the window when I saw Josh's car pull up outside. My heart lurched in the same old way at the sight of his familiar figure getting out of it, and I was almost annoyed with him for coming back and starting it all up again. But of course, he was only going to pick up his stuff, wasn't he?

'Hi, Mel, how's everything?' He'd obviously seen me looking out of the kitchen window, where I'd been standing nursing a mug of coffee, and came round to the back door.

'Fine, Josh, thanks. And you?'

'Yeah, great.' He nodded, sniffing the air. 'Wow, that coffee smells good. Not that I'm dropping hints of course. But if you were to offer ... ' His eyes twinkled as he perched his hip on the edge of the table and swung a long leg.

I laughed and reached for the kettle. 'Idiot! It's only instant. That OK?'

'Lovely. So what have you been doing since I saw you last?' He accepted his coffee with a nod of thanks, as I joined him at the table.

'Oh, I had a little trip. I went up to London and stayed for a long weekend with Sam.'

'Ah, yes. I remember you saying you might do that.'

He did? From all that time ago? How amazing.

'And did you have a good time?' The formal remark was so unlike his previous banter that I glanced at him in surprise. The smile had vanished and his expression had darkened.

'Mmm, yes. Yes I did. I would have liked to stay longer but Sam couldn't get any more time off.'

'So, what does he do for his work, your Sam?' Josh enquired, lifting his gaze to my face.

I felt my brows arch in surprise. 'Oh, Sam's a girl, not a 'he'!' I laughed. 'Her full name's Samantha.'

'A girl?' Josh's eyes were wide with astonishment as he looked into mine. 'But . . . you never said, and I assumed . . . '

'You never asked!' I retorted in surprise.

'Oh, I see.' He paused, looking down at his coffee as he swirled it round and round. 'So, what about . . . um . . . who's that David bloke, then?' He glanced up at me with a glimmer of amusement. 'He's definitely not a girl, from what I saw of him. And he certainly didn't behave like one!'

I felt warmth flood my cheeks and the smile slid from my face. 'David is a long story, Josh, and belongs firmly in

303

the past. Maybe I'll tell you about him sometime. But right now, I think, if you're ready, we'll go and get your things from the office.'

I spoke abruptly as my last remark brought it home to me that of course I would never tell Josh the story of David, because he wouldn't be here to listen to it.

'Sure, OK. No problem.' He nodded, then not meeting my eyes, he said in a casual, throwaway tone, 'So you're not . . . er . . . attached, then? There isn't . . . er . . . anyone special in your life?'

But at that moment Josh's mobile rang with a text message tone, and I jumped at the sudden noise. He put down his empty mug and pulled the phone from his jeans pocket.

He scrolled down the text, gave a low whistle and jumped to his feet. 'Sorry, Mel, something's come up. I have to go into the office.' He crammed the phone back into his pocket as he spoke, and was already heading for the door. 'I'll be back later for that stuff. See you then.'

He was gone before I could draw breath to reply. Wondering what it could be that was so urgent, I shrugged and sighed as I carried the empty mugs over to the sink.

★   ★   ★

I didn't see Josh again until the following day. I was in the lounge, sorting through a pile of old newspapers and magazines that had accumulated in the overflowing rack.

'Hi, Josh.' I smiled briefly as his face appeared around the door, and turned to put the newer stuff back in the rack again.

'How are things?' He entered the room, whistling under his breath, his hands in his pockets as he hovered awkwardly beside me.

'All right, I suppose.' The old ones for throwing out were in my arms as I turned and shrugged, wondering at this stilted approach. 'And you?'

'Yeah, fine. Very much so, actually.' Whistling tunelessly, he strolled across to the window and stood looking out.

'Oh, why's that, then?' Curious, I gave him my full attention.

'I've had some good news.' As he turned and took a few steps towards me, I saw the elation in his face.

My heart gave a lurch and began to thud wildly.

A beaming smile spread across his face.

I dropped the newspapers to the floor with a thump. 'Well?'

Josh seized my hand and pulled me down to sit beside him. His eyes dancing with excitement, he drew a deep breath.

'Mel, not only has the company given the contract to Cornwall, you know that already. But on the back of it, I've got my promotion! And a salary to match it as well!' He grinned.

'Oh, Josh that's wonderful!' I could feel a smile as broad as his, stretching across my own face. 'I am just so pleased for you, I really am!'

'Thank you,' he said simply. 'Oh, Mel, I'm over the moon about this.' He squeezed my hand. 'And about something else too.' His expression had become more serious as he looked deep into my eyes.

'Oh?' I queried, waiting for Josh to explain.

But he didn't. Instead, he released my hand and stood up.

'Just — just stay right where you are for a minute, Mel. Don't move — I'll be right back.' And he hurried from the room.

Bemused, I did as I was told, and he was back almost immediately.

The beaming smile was still on his face and there was such an air of excitement about him, I felt my eyes widen in surprise. I also noticed he was holding one hand behind his back.

Then like a conjuror producing a rabbit from a hat, he whipped his arm around to the front and, with a theatrical flourish, presented me with a sheaf of the most beautiful lilies I had ever seen. White and powder pink, the dew still fresh on their velvety petals, they filled the room with fragrance. Together with the ferns surrounding them, I thought wistfully, they looked just like a bridal bouquet.

I know my jaw dropped as I goggled incredulously from Josh to the flowers and back again. 'F . . . for me?'

He nodded and thrust them into my arms.

'But why?' I buried my nose in a golden centre and took in the heavenly aroma.

'Because,' his eyes held mine as I looked up, 'today is a day of celebration.'

'Oh?' I stared blankly back. 'Yes, we're celebrating your promotion, I know. But I still don't understand why . . . '

'Come and sit down.' With a touch on my arm, Josh gently took the bouquet and placed it on a side table, before joining me on the settee again.

'Mel, I have so much to tell you I hardly know how to start.' He paused and took a deep breath.

'The beginning is always a good place,' I prompted gently, then waited.

'Yes. Well, up to now I've never told you much about my private life and I know you've been too polite to ask questions.'

'Oh, well . . . I . . . '

He raised a hand. 'No, I understand. But now Mel, I'm in a position to explain everything.'

Josh ran a hand through his hair in the familiar endearing gesture, then turned to me.

'I believe I told you I had a long-term girlfriend, partner, whatever, when I was younger, didn't I?'

I nodded, hanging on his every word. 'Yes, you did.'

'Well, I loved her with all my heart and I thought she loved me, too. But our relationship began to deteriorate rapidly when she found I was going to give up the running and all the media attention it brought. To her, as well as me.

'We started having rows, just over silly little things. At the beginning I made excuses for her change of mood, putting it down to women's problems, pressure of work, anything to justify her behaviour. I was blind to what was going on, Mel, because I didn't want to see it.'

'You're not the first man that's happened to.' I patted his arm sympathetically.

Josh shrugged. 'So I went along with it for a while. It took me a long time to dawn on me that she'd been taking me for a ride, and what an utter fool I'd been not to have seen it sooner. I'd loved her so much, but she was only interested in revelling in the limelight.'

'In the end she walked out on me. And I was so mad at myself for being used.' Josh looked down at his hands, resting on his knees, and sighed.

'Quite honestly Mel, it almost broke

my heart. And I've never looked at another girl since. I suppose I was too afraid of making a fool of myself again, even when the opportunities were there.'

He looked up as he reached for my hand. 'Until now, that is.' His other hand reached out and folded over mine. 'Now that I'm certain of my future I can tell you at last what I've been longing to say for months.'

His expression softened, and warmth crept into his sparkling eyes. 'That I've loved you Mel from the very first moment I stepped over the threshold of this house, and you told me to strip off my clothes!'

Love? I stared at him open-mouthed. Had I heard him correctly? Josh . . . did he say . . . he loved me? I gazed up in wonderment at those glorious eyes, fixed now in a steady gaze on mine. The burning intensity in them, and the arms which now reached out to wrap me close, told me all I wanted to know. I was convinced beyond doubt that my wildest dreams really were about to come true.

Josh's warm lips now came down on mine in a kiss so gentle, yet so firm, becoming more passionate by the second, that the room swayed about me as I returned his love with every fibre of my being.

The kiss lasted a long time, while feelings of the most delicious kind ran up and down my spine.

At last I tore myself away and laid my head against Josh's chest, where I could feel his heart thudding under my cheek. And as he gently stroked my hair, I gazed up at his familiar face, the face that had haunted my anguished dreams for so long, the face I knew as well as my own.

'Oh, Josh . . . I never knew you felt that way about me . . . never dreamt . . . And I had a bad time like you did, over David. I thought I'd lost all faith in men too, after him. But deep-down I've loved you too, right from the very start, but I could never show it because

. . . you just didn't seem interested.'

His grasp tightened. 'Mel, I had no idea . . . ' Josh slowly shook his head. 'But that was only because I thought that David . . . and then Sam . . . I thought you were surrounded by men! Oh my darling, I was so mixed up.'

As I felt his grasp tighten I sighed with contentment.

'And looking back, I realise I've got a lot to apologise for too.'

My head jerked up.

'Apologise? Oh, Josh, what for? There isn't anything . . . '

'But yes, there is! My moods, my tempers — I was horrible to you at times. But underneath, it was only because I thought I didn't stand a chance with you.'

'It doesn't matter.' I relaxed into his arms again. 'I thought those moods were all to do with the pressure of your work. But really, none of that matters any more.'

'No, I suppose it doesn't,' Josh murmured, 'and now we're free at last

Mel, free to spend the rest of our lives together. If you'd like to, that is!'

After we'd both burst out laughing together, we stayed where we were for a long time. And when we roused ourselves at last, we left the room, hands linked, to find the others and share our good news.